G R JORDAN

Cinderella's Carriage

A Highlands and Islands Detective Thriller #39

Fairytales are more than true: not
because they tell us that dragons exist,
but because they tell us dragons can
be beaten.

NEIL GAIMEN

Contents

Foreword   iii
Acknowledgments   iv
Books by G R Jordan   v
Chapter 01   1
Chapter 02   11
Chapter 03   19
Chapter 04   27
Chapter 05   36
Chapter 06   45
Chapter 07   53
Chapter 08   62
Chapter 09   71
Chapter 10   80
Chapter 11   89
Chapter 12   97
Chapter 13   106
Chapter 14   115
Chapter 15   124
Chapter 16   133
Chapter 17   142
Chapter 18   151
Chapter 19   160
Chapter 20   168
Chapter 21   176

Chapter 22	185
Chapter 23	195
Chapter 24	204
Chapter 25	212
Read on to discover the Patrick Smythe series!	222
About the Author	225
Also by G R Jordan	227

Foreword

The events of this book, while based around real and also fictitious locations around Scotland, are entirely fictional and all characters do not represent any living or deceased person. All companies are fictitious representations. And if you ever see a woman in a tartan shawl and trews chasing a carriage, simply step aside: it's for the best!

Acknowledgments

To Ken, Jean, Colin, Evelyn, John and Rosemary for your work in bringing this novel to completion, your time and effort is deeply appreciated.

Books by G R Jordan

The Highlands and Islands Detective series (Crime)

1. Water's Edge
2. The Bothy
3. The Horror Weekend
4. The Small Ferry
5. Dead at Third Man
6. The Pirate Club
7. A Personal Agenda
8. A Just Punishment
9. The Numerous Deaths of Santa Claus
10. Our Gated Community
11. The Satchel
12. Culhwch Alpha
13. Fair Market Value
14. The Coach Bomber
15. The Culling at Singing Sands
16. Where Justice Fails
17. The Cortado Club
18. Cleared to Die
19. Man Overboard!
20. Antisocial Behaviour
21. Rogues' Gallery
22. The Death of Macleod - Inferno Book 1

23. A Common Man - Inferno Book 2
24. A Sweeping Darkness - Inferno Book 3
25. Dormie 5
26. The First Minister - Past Mistakes Book 1
27. The Guilty Parties - Past Mistakes Book 2
28. Vengeance is Mine - Past Mistakes Book 3
29. Winter Slay Bells
30. Macleod's Cruise
31. Scrambled Eggs
32. The Esoteric Tear
33. A Rock 'n' Roll Murder
34. The Slaughterhouse
35. Boomtown
36. The Absent Sculptor
37. A Trip to Rome
38. A Time to Rest
39. Cinderella's Carriage
40. Wild Swimming

Kirsten Stewart Thrillers (Thriller)

1. A Shot at Democracy
2. The Hunted Child
3. The Express Wishes of Mr MacIver
4. The Nationalist Express
5. The Hunt for 'Red Anna'
6. The Execution of Celebrity
7. The Man Everyone Wanted
8. Busman's Holiday

9. A Personal Favour
10. Infiltrator
11. Implosion
12. Traitor

Jac Moonshine Thrillers

1. Jac's Revenge
2. Jac for the People
3. Jac the Pariah

Siobhan Duffy Mysteries

1. A Giant Killing
2. Death of the Witch
3. The Bloodied Hands
4. A Hermit's Death

The Contessa Munroe Mysteries (Cozy Mystery)

1. Corpse Reviver
2. Frostbite
3. Cobra's Fang

The Patrick Smythe Series (Crime)

1. The Disappearance of Russell Hadleigh

2. The Graves of Calgary Bay
3. The Fairy Pools Gathering

Austerley & Kirkgordon Series (Fantasy)

1. Crescendo!
2. The Darkness at Dillingham
3. Dagon's Revenge
4. Ship of Doom

Supernatural and Elder Threat Assessment Agency (SETAA) Series (Fantasy)

1. Scarlett O'Meara: Beastmaster

Island Adventures Series (Cosy Fantasy Adventure)

1. Surface Tensions

Dark Wen Series (Horror Fantasy)

1. The Blasphemous Welcome
2. The Demon's Chalice

Chapter 01

The view from the garden centre had never looked more stunning. Clarissa sat in the leather chair, staring like she was marvelling at some terrific sculpture or a rare jewel. It had snowed the week before, heavy and thick, and as usual caused the season's havoc with the roads.

But now everyone was used to it. The gritters and the snowploughs had done their work, and Inverness was moving again. But no snowplough or gritter had been near this view. The mountains looked resplendent in white, almost like a baby wrapped up in a christening shawl.

The sky had been overcast earlier on in the day, but now the clouds had lifted a bit, yet the temperature was still so very cold. The snow wasn't melting and for that, Clarissa was glad. She didn't have to work today. She didn't have to work now until New Year. This was the run into Christmas, the penultimate week, and she was going to spend it with Frank.

She'd had words with Macleod recently, explained to him she needed the time off. She'd done her fair share. Sabine could handle any routine inquiries. And it was the arts world—things would keep. It wasn't like being on the murder team. It wasn't a case of 'you had to get there and investigate straight away.' And besides, how many art thefts were there at this time of year? Few of the ilk that Clarissa was involved in. No, she was having two weeks, minimum. And she was starting today.

Frank was wrapped up in a large coat, and Clarissa waved her hand at him. 'Would you take that thing off? It's warm in here.'

'It's bloody freezing outside,' said Frank.

'We're not outside, are we?'

'You still have your shawl on.'

'The shawl isn't for the cold. It's a fashion item. It's not about being warm,' said Clarissa.

This wasn't entirely true, of course. The shawl was an incredible source of heat during this wintertime, and she had a slightly lighter one for the summer. But the shawl *was* a fashion item. Some people said it was the heart and soul of Clarissa, but that wasn't true. She was much more than that.

'I won't tell you again. Take your coat off.'

Frank sighed, stood up, undid his coat, and put it around the chair he had been sitting on, before sitting back down and looking at the mince pie in front of him. It was then he licked his lips. Clarissa knew Frank liked mince pies, but more than that, he liked to have brandy sauce over it. It wasn't proper brandy here in the sauce that you'd worry about driving afterwards. But it was good to see a smile on his face.

The golf course was closed, so he wasn't working at the moment anyway, and it looked like it would be closed for the next two weeks, so heavy was the snow. So Frank had taken his time off as well.

'I thought we'd do some of the Christmas shopping this afternoon,' said Clarissa. 'Then after that, we'd sit in tonight.'

'Sounds good,' said Frank.

He wasn't difficult to please. He liked nothing more than just sitting in with her, cuddling up on the sofa. Clarissa found they didn't even talk that much. They could just sit there. They watched sport together too. It was a side of Clarissa that most people didn't know—she watched sport. After all, she was competitive. Back in her day, she played lacrosse better than anyone, although that was some time ago.

'This pie's good. We'll come here again,' said Frank.

Clarissa smiled at him. He liked his food and so did she. And that was life with them, really—out to the theatre, out to shows, out to restaurants. There was enough money between them. They weren't lavish; they weren't extravagant, but they both worked hard in their life, both without kids. She had enough put by, so had Frank, and they were going to enjoy it.

She looked out through the window again. *Breathtaking*, she thought. *Breathtaking*.

She reached down for the coffee in front of her. They were sitting in the main restaurant of the garden centre, close to the window, and at this time of year, it was busy. As most garden centres did now, plants were only a part of what was on offer.

There was the Christmas selection. Everywhere you went, there were dancing gizmos, penguins singing at you, reindeer nodding their heads, and animatronic animals here and there. An abundance of tinsel was for sale, Christmas trees, and of course, the obligatory Santa's grotto was ready for the kids.

Of course, Clarissa never went near Santa's grotto. All those kids standing, and then half of them crying when they came out, disappointed with what they'd got. She couldn't be bothered by that. She was here in the quiet corner—or as quiet as it ever got corner—of the restaurant. The restaurant was heaving though with people coming for their Christmas lunch. She wondered if it was just friends meeting up, work dos, who knew?

She had thought about taking the team out. Patterson was going to be working over Christmas. Sabine was covering Glasgow. They wouldn't be in on Christmas Day, of course, or Boxing Day. The arts team never came in on those public holidays unless there was something on. There was no need. But Sabine and Patterson would be on call. Clarissa wouldn't. And unless they nicked the crown jewels, she was off scot-free.

She lifted the coffee to her lips again, took a very satisfying drink, put it back down and glanced around the restaurant. It was then she saw him.

Detective Chief Inspector Seoras Macleod—or as Clarissa and some of the rest of them called him, the Big Boss—was now making his way across the restaurant. The name was well deserved for he ran her department, Hope McGrath's murder team, and was rumoured to be taking more teams under his wing. Clarissa watched as he moved through the mass of people. Seoras was polite, especially when he wasn't operating as the chief inspector.

If he was taking control of the press, or if he was having to manhandle a suspect, or make things happen in the case, he could be very direct. Incredibly blunt, almost to a point of rudeness, and in truth, Clarissa was impressed by that. But here amongst the public, Seoras wasn't at his best.

He was carefully trying to make his way round, dancing past what looked like a five- or six-year-old. Seoras seemed to have the belief that the six-year-old would respond and, in some sort of mutual effort, they would find a way past each other. It was quite clear to Clarissa that the six-year-old was completely oblivious to what Macleod was doing.

He almost fell over the child. Seoras then spent time apologising to the mother. He seemed to take great offence, though, that she'd let her kid run out in front of him, and then stand there and not deal with the situation.

Clarissa turned back to her coffee and took another sip. She hadn't seen Jane. Jane was Macleod's partner. If Macleod was in a garden centre, Jane should be with him. Seoras was not a man who frequented a garden centre on his own. If he'd come for coffee, it wouldn't be here; it would be back in town. He had his favourite shop, his coffee shop that he always went to, or at least when he was in the area. He was fussy about his coffee, far more than Clarissa, although she liked the good stuff.

She scanned the rest of the crowd, wondering if maybe Hope was around. Hope had received some good news recently, and in truth, Clarissa was happy for her. Clarissa and Hope were getting on better than they ever had—*two women no longer in the same kitchen*, Clarissa thought.

It had been tough working with Hope. It didn't help that she was six feet tall, but strikingly good looking, brave, and courageous, and could do things by the book. The bigwigs loved her. Macleod loved her too. But Clarissa could see that he'd brought her on. Macleod wasn't someone who used her or put her up on a pedestal. Macleod had taught her the art of detective work. And he'd done a good job.

Clarissa had a slightly different reputation with the bigwigs. She went 'off on one' at times, as Macleod put it. But going off on one had saved his life, on one occasion at least. He never criticised her in that sense. In truth, she thought Macleod saw what she was, and how best to defend her.

She wasn't bitter about that. But Seoras could get in under your skin, capable, despite how rough around the edges you could be, of making you fit into the place that he needed you. She scanned the crowd again. No Jane.

First, she looked back at Frank. He was almost through his mince pie by now, for he didn't hold back when he got something he liked. He hadn't held back when he'd seen her.

Her family had thought she might like to marry a viscount, an earl, or a laird of the land. Somebody high-up, wherever it be. Preferably Scotland, of course. That was home. But she'd ended up marrying the man who looked after the golf course. And while it was a decent club, it wasn't the most prestigious one, by a long stretch. She had found in Frank somebody she could just be herself with, and somebody she could care for without feeling burdened by it. As she stared at Frank, she felt incredibly lucky. Right until she heard the voice in her ear.

'Sorry to interrupt you. Oh, hello, Frank.'

Clarissa turned her head and looked up at the big boss. 'Seoras,' said Clarissa. 'Absolute delight. I've told you this, Frank. No matter where I go, he needs to be there for me. I've told you this, Frank. He can't leave me alone. First day of the holidays. Where is he? Right here with us. It's barely gone half past ten.'

'Did you get the mince pies?' said Frank. 'They're superb. You need one with the brandy sauce.'

'Oh, I'm sure Seoras has got lots to do that doesn't involve being around here,' said Clarissa. 'That's right, isn't it, Seoras?'

Macleod shook his head. 'I'm going to need a seat,' he said.

'I'll go for a wander,' said Frank.

'No, you bloody won't,' said Clarissa. 'You sit there. I'm sure there's a seat he can draw over.'

Frank looked with a tinge of shock at Clarissa. 'What?' she said. 'I'm not on the clock now. You don't have to get out of the way for him. This is my time. This is my holiday.'

'About that,' said Macleod. He turned and grabbed an empty chair, pulled it up to the table before sitting down.

'No,' she said.

'What do you mean "no?"' said Macleod.

'No.'

'The chief constable's been tapped by a friend. He wants somebody to look into this. And if it's the chief constable—'

'Jim. Tell Jim to go and—'

'No,' said Macleod. 'Not Jim. The chief constable. Not the assistant. The—'

'I don't care,' said Clarissa. 'Sabine can handle it. Sabine knows the art world as well as I do. That's why she's in the remote office. Tell him to get hold of Sabine. Get her to do a face-to-face call with him. You know, one of the video ones. He'll be quite happy once he sees Sabine. He'll prefer it to seeing my old mug.'

'There's nothing wrong with your old mug,' said Frank defensively.

'Thank you, dear,' said Clarissa. 'But when it comes to those people, I know where I am.'

'No, you don't,' said Macleod. 'He wants you.'

'What do you mean, "He wants me?"'

'He's been tapped by a friend for you to investigate a disappearance. It's a priceless carriage that's been taken.'

'I don't care if the king's had his nicked; I will not look for it!'

'It's a small one, a tiny piece, but it's part of a collection,' said Macleod.

'Seoras, why are you still talking? No! I'm on holiday. Sabine can handle it, and if she says she can't, then I'll talk to her and tell her how to handle it. I am having my time off with Frank.'

'We have a lot planned,' said Frank.

'There, see,' said Clarissa, giving Frank a smile. 'We have a lot planned. No.'

'It's part of the Cinderella collection,' said Macleod.

It wasn't often that Clarissa ever gave a sharp intake of breath. Very little surprised her. However, she drew in breath like it was going out of fashion. 'Cinderella collection?' said Clarissa.

'Yeah, apparently the small one's been taken. Apparently—' Macleod stopped because Clarissa was on her feet.

'Was Patterson in the office?'

'He was going off to that Christmas—'

'Oh, that's right. Yes, he was, wasn't he? Is that the main one in town?'

'Yes, Church of Scotland, in the city centre.'

'Bingo,' said Clarissa. She already had the shawl on, but she grabbed her handbag, flung it over her shoulder, and then briefly stopped. She spun round to Frank. 'Sorry, dear. I've got to go.'

'Okay,' said Frank. Clarissa turned away, but Frank called after her. 'When will I see you?'

'When it's done,' she said. 'Just as soon as it's done.'

She went to tear off, and then she stopped again. She turned back. 'Tape the rugby!' And then, Clarissa was gone.

'You said something about a mince pie and brandy sauce?' said Macleod.

'Yeah,' said Frank. 'Get me another one while you're at it.'

Clarissa was out of the garden centre like a whippet, and only when she reached the car did she feel the vibration of the phone in her pocket. She picked it up, looked at it and saw some details from Macleod. There was an address to go to in the Cairngorms, but there was also beside this a request to keep the whole thing as quiet as possible. That made sense . . . the Cinderella collection.

Six carriages, varying in size, a jewel in each. But where were they? She knew about them, but some were with private collectors. Some were unknown.

The little green car sped through the city centre, and she parked up outside a Christmas carol service, where she could hear the singing inside. 'O Little Town of Bethlehem' was being belted out as she entered through the rear door. She stopped in the middle of the transept, looking left and right for Patterson. He was in the middle of the pews, about three-quarters of the way back. Everyone was standing at the moment, singing the last few lines of the carol.

Clarissa reached the pew line Patterson sat in, just as everyone sat down.

'Pats,' she whispered, but not in the quietest of voices. 'Job, need to go.' Patterson looked over, his face almost in shock.

'Shh! He's about to do his—'

'I'm sorry, ma'am,' said Clarissa. 'This is police business. Pats, we need to go.'

Patterson reluctantly turned in his chair and picked up his raincoat, shuffled along the pew, causing consternation. Clarissa looked up towards the front, where a minister had taken to the pulpit. She could see he was about to speak, but then he looked over at her. His eyes were focused, and she thought if ever hellfire could come down from a pulpit, it would come from that one.

Patterson reached the end of the pew, and Clarissa slapped

him on the back. 'Let's get moving, Pats,' she said. She spun round with alacrity, looked up at the minister in the pulpit. 'Sorry to disturb you. Merry Christmas to everyone! Happy New Year!' And as she marched down the aisle, called out loudly, 'I hope Santa's good to everyone!'

Patterson's face was bright red as they left the church.

Chapter 02

'But Pats, don't you get it? It's the Cinderella carriages. Yes? I mean, these things are—they're legend in some ways. There are rumours of one coming out at Christmas in the big parade in the city centre. But the others, so little is known; they're hidden away, a lot of them. They're with collectors. These are the Cinderella carriages. These are something else.'

'That was the carol service. I told Macleod I wanted to go to it. He gave me time away, okay? He said he could cover me for a couple of hours.'

'And he did,' said Clarissa. 'He came and got me. I mean, this is . . . big. You've got to understand that, Pats. This is really huge.'

'I just wanted a bit of time, okay? I'm on call for Christmas. I could get called in. This was my time to sit and have my Christmas. And you just marched in—'

'You're on call,' said Clarissa.

'And what, you couldn't have waited half an hour? You couldn't have waited for the service to finish?'

'Hey, it's a case. We're on it. You get going. Come on, Pats. You know that.'

Clarissa shouted the last sentence because the noise as she drove along was almost deafening. She hadn't put the hood up. Instead, the cold air was whipping around the car. But she seemed all right, almost invigorated. Patterson, on the other hand, was wrapped up in his coat, gloves, scarf, and even a beanie hat.

'Get better headwear,' said Clarissa. Her hair, thin as it was, was being buffeted about, but her cheeks were rosy. There was a life about her she hadn't felt in a while.

'It's out in the Cairngorms,' said Pats. 'You could have waited half an hour. We could have been just twenty minutes late. It wouldn't have been a problem.'

'Shush,' said Clarissa as loudly as she could. 'Now listen up. Apparently, we're going to be met by somebody at this address. We can't talk about this, okay? We can't make it too public. The people who own this stuff, they don't—'

'They just called the police in. What do you mean we can't make it too public? They've lost something; it's gone and we're going to investigate,' said Pats.

'No, no, no! We've been asked to look at it by the Chief Constable.'

'Why?' asked Patterson.

'It's a favour. Macleod said it was a favour for whoever this person is. And when the Chief Constable asks for favours, you get it done, okay? That's why I prioritised this. Anyway, you can go to another carol service.'

'I wanted that one,' said Patterson.

'Why?'

'Doesn't matter,' he said.

Clarissa sat beside him, looking out to the road and then back to Patterson again. It mattered.

'Why?' she said.

'I kind of get thankful, especially at this time of year. I'm still here,' he said, almost too quietly for her to hear. Clarissa put her indicator on and pulled over into a lay-by that came up sharply. She engaged the handbrake and turned to face Patterson.

'Thankful?' she whispered.

'When they cut my throat, I didn't think I'd be here. When it comes to this time of year—and some others—I like to go to the church. I like to say thanks,' he breathed. 'I say thank you for you. You saved my life. It's what I do. You have to be thankful for things like that. Thankful for second chances.'

Clarissa looked away for a moment, and then back to Patterson. 'I'm sorry,' she said. 'I didn't realise. If I'd thought—'

'Not your strong point,' said Patterson. 'You're a woman of action. You see something, you do it; you don't always think, but I'm still glad you're about.'

She gave a nod, turned, started the engine up again, and dropped the handbrake. Within thirty seconds, they were again racing along towards the Cairngorms.

The Cairngorms looked magnificent, with snow on all sides. Since the snow ploughs had been through, the A9 was well cleared. However, as you moved further up into the mountain, some roads were more treacherous. But it was snow that had fallen; it had compacted well and it wasn't ice. Clarissa knew how to drive on this surface, and they arrived smoothly at a small holding.

It could only have been twenty acres, but there was a log cabin in the middle. As they approached the gate, there was no intercom, and Patterson jumped out, undoing the gate, allowing the car through. He closed the gate behind him, and

Clarissa took the car up the barely visible path in front of the log house.

Once there, they got out together and approached the front door. There was a large brass knocker, and Clarissa thundered hard on it and turned to look around. Snow lay on the trees. She could see where a bird had hopped across the patio at the front of the log cabin, leaving its thin footprints in the snow. Clarissa smiled. She liked Christmas but there was also something else fired up inside of her. The Cinderella carriage. This would be good.

The door opened, and Clarissa stood looking at a woman of a fine frame. Her hair wasn't long, more like a messy bob. The hair mushroomed almost so it didn't look like the demure 1920s cut, but more like a mop on top of her head. And yet she was smart with it, black trousers and a jacket that—what on earth was that?

It looked like it was made from a type of leaf. Bullrushes, that's what it reminded her of. Well, that was American, wasn't it? Bullrush? We just had rushes. She had to think for a moment. It was rather a neat coat, though, and she wondered if she had it commissioned.

'Can I help you?' said the young woman. She could only have been early twenties at most.

'My name's Detective Inspector Clarissa Urquhart. This is DC Patterson. We've been asked to talk to you about the disappearance of some items.'

Clarissa held up her warrant card before putting it back underneath her shawl.

'Welcome,' said the woman. 'My employer is Mr Garrick. Unfortunately, he's not here at the moment. He had business out of the country, but I will help you. My name is Laura Silver and we have indeed had a theft. Please, please come in.'

Clarissa stepped inside the small house and waited for Laura to close the door. She then let the woman pass, allowing herself to be led, but leaned over to Patterson to whisper in his ear, 'Garrick is an underworld collector; a serious underworld collector.'

Laura showed them into a cosy-looking living room. Everything was pristine. There was a drinks cabinet and Clarissa clocked the whiskies that were in it. There was no way she could afford that, never mind the quality of liquor that was inside it. She thought she recognised the rug on the floor that and could put a price tag on of several thousand pounds without even hesitating. One of the paintings on the wall she knew was at least a hundred thousand. Pats was probably missing all of this.

'It went from here,' said Laura, pointing to a table.

The table was clearly a one-off, made of mainly glass and had several levels to it, presumably to display items. Either side of the centre, on different levels, were a couple of crystal-cut decanters. The quality of them was unbelievable. And though it wasn't her field, Clarissa would have expected the price to be well beyond her salary for the next ten years.

'It was one of the carriages, the ones incorrectly known as the Cinderella carriages,' said Laura.

'I've heard of them,' said Clarissa. 'I've seen a photograph of some of them. Which one was this one?'

'This was the smallest.'

'The smallest?' said Patterson.

Clarissa turned to her colleague. 'The Cinderella carriages, Pats, are basically a collection of six different carriages. They're exquisitely made of gold and precious stones. They are unbelievable. This first one is tiny. You could put it in your hand. There's a jewel that sits inside of it, and this one probably is the most expensive.' She looked at Laura.

'It's hard to value them,' said Laura. 'My employer, Mr Garrick, paid a small fortune for it.'

'Excuse me a moment,' said Patterson. 'I don't understand something.'

'Well, what is it?' asked Laura.

'You pay a small fortune for this, and I'm assuming that lots of the other items in here are worth quite a bit. We just walked in through the gate. I can't see much of a security system. I see nothing stopping anyone from coming in here and taking any of this.'

'Nobody knows it's here,' said Clarissa suddenly.

'What?' said Pats.

'The Detective Inspector's correct. The greatest security you can put on an item is that no one knows where it is. Mr Garrick does not advertise his houses. When you pass by this house,' said Laura, 'you would not have identified it as the house of a man worth probably billions.'

'Well, you got me there,' said Patterson. 'Even so, I'd have thought—'

'Mr Garrick isn't one of these people who likes a lot of security. Mr Garrick likes to remain unknown, except to those in the field of collecting. His businesses run with him operating several deep layers above. Most of the people working for him don't even know they work for him,' said Laura. 'Mr Garrick operates secretly. It's what works for him.'

'And why we were told to not say anything about where we were going. And why I wasn't given a name,' said Clarissa.

'Exactly,' said Laura. 'Please keep this all quiet.'

'Do you have any video footage?' asked Clarissa.

'I do. But it's very slow. We use it really for being able to make sure that nobody's been in when I'm not here. But I'm afraid it won't help.'

'If you show it, we'll judge that,' said Clarissa. The pair were taken through to a small room, a corridor away, where they were sat before a screen.

'The system runs automatically. I don't have access to it normally, but Mr Garrick's given me access. That's the essence of the situation. If you notice the time stamp, basically the system goes down for twenty minutes, and the item disappears.'

Clarissa looked at the pictures. For all intents and purposes, there was a completely still image, and then suddenly the item vanished before the still image remained without the item.

'Mr Garrick wasn't here?'

'Regretfully, no, and I wasn't here either. I was allowed a day off. When I came back, this is what happened. I had to inform Mr Garrick, who was not well pleased, and asked me to inform your Chief Constable.'

'If I may,' said Patterson, 'I'm sure you could employ people to find this item.'

'We could,' said Laura. 'But Mr Garrick said he has a good relationship with your Chief Constable and that, well, you could keep it quiet while still investigating. You could also hand it back without naming Mr Garrick.'

'That'll be up to the Chief Constable,' said Clarissa before Patterson could speak. She wasn't sure that this was completely suitable form, but at the top end, things happened, not necessarily illegally, but sometimes things had to operate in a smoother fashion.

'Do you know anybody who wants this item?' asked Clarissa.

'With all due respect, Detective Inspector Urquhart, Mr Garrick asked for you. And he asked for you for a reason. There are plenty of people who would want this item. Plenty of people around the world. But he said to me, you were the most dogged he'd ever find. And so, that's why he asked for you.'

'Well, thank you,' said Clarissa. 'I may be back for further questions. Are you planning on going anywhere?'

'You can reach me at this number. Please do call ahead because I'm not always here. I have other functions to do for Mr Garrick. But obviously, I'll make myself available if ever you call.'

'That's much appreciated,' said Clarissa. 'It's a great shame. It's a beautiful piece, I hear.'

'Quite something,' said Laura Silver, escorting them to the door. 'And remember, please go quietly.'

They walked back to the car, and for a moment Clarissa sat there thinking.

'Are you sure you're up to this?' said Patterson.

'What's that mean, Pats?' said Clarissa sharply.

'She told you to go quietly.'

Clarissa didn't answer, but simply punched Patterson in the arm.

Chapter 03

Clarissa sat down at her desk, breathing heavily. She'd almost bounded back up into the office, her mind running through ideas about what she needed to do. The first thing was to get the team together. She made a call down to Glasgow, finding Ferguson in the office, and told her to get up north, along with Emmett. As much as she wanted this case for herself, she knew she needed the team around her. There'd be a lot to look at. Patterson sat down across from her, and she lifted her head to pass on her instructions.

'Patterson, I want you to get on to finding out where Garrick is. If somebody's nicked this item, they need to know where he's had it. You heard Laura Silver. She said that this was one of his private homes. Nobody knows it's there.'

'Well, she knew it was there,' said Pats.

'Exactly,' said Clarissa. 'Some people will know. Find out where he's been. Find out where he's been travelling.'

'You realise that this is a man who shrouds himself in secrecy?'

'Well, un-secret it,' said Clarissa. 'You need to find out where he's been. I'll give you a few numbers to call as well. He still has to make his deals. He's a collector. People will know.'

'And maybe,' said Pats, 'you think somebody will actually tie in with where he's been?'

'I don't know, but at the moment all we've got is a carriage that disappeared. We've got film footage that says it was there and then it wasn't. Whoever broke into the house may have tampered with the video feed. In truth, it didn't look that difficult to do.'

'Laura never explained that fully, did she?' said Pats.

'Looked like an old system. I mean, there's no protection up there for that item.'

'No, there wasn't, was there? It's very cavalier.'

'No, it's not, Pats. It's a very clever ploy. I'm not sure he's had much stolen before. He will have houses that people know about, but this is one that people didn't know about, and that's deliberate. He'll keep some of his best stuff there.'

'It didn't look like much from the outside, did it? Not a very grandiose estate,' said Patterson.

'And that's the point,' said Clarissa. 'Get with it, Pats; come on.'

The adrenaline was pumping inside her, even though she had next to nothing to work on. She would try to find the owners of the rest of the carriages. Some would be known; some would be harder to track down. She'd have to discover when the carriages were last purchased.

She placed a call to an old trader down in Coventry. He was good, kept an eye on the market, and knew when items were traded. He said that most of the carriages could be traced, but he'd need half an hour. Clarissa was quite happy about that.

She also rang up the organising committee for the Inverness Christmas Parade. She'd heard rumours there was going to be a carriage in it, and she wondered if it was the carriage. Pulling a book off the shelf which detailed a little of the history of the Cinderella carriages, Clarissa scanned it while waiting for the phone to answer.

The carriages were surrounded in mystery, and who built them still remained an issue. Someone said it was a Russian; others had said it was someone from the Balkan states. Whatever had happened to them, they had passed through royalty on their way before coming onto the open market. They weren't easy to move about, and the largest of them being put on display in the Inverness Parade would be a massive coup for the city.

'Hello, you've got through to Annie. How can I help you?'

'This is Detective Inspector Clarissa Urquhart. I'm looking to find out about your parade. There's a flyer talking about a grand carriage being in the parade. You've said it's a Cinderella's carriage. Is it an actual Cinderella's carriage?'

'Well, it doesn't turn back into a pumpkin at midnight,' said Annie.

'No, no, you misunderstand me,' said Clarissa. 'I'm looking to see if it's one of the six.'

'I'm afraid you've lost me there,' said Annie. 'To be honest, this has to do with Hamper Holdings. They're supplying the carriage. Apparently, it's quite an arty one—that's really what I know. They've been very good to us this year, sponsoring the parade. I've seen pictures of the carriage.'

'You don't happen to have any of those pictures, do you?' asked Clarissa.

'I do.'

'Send them through to me, please, if you would. And also, who are you dealing with in Hamper Holdings?'

'Well, I've been dealing with a lot of the underlings. But if you really want any details,' said Annie, 'you need to speak to Isabel McNeice. She's the owner of Hamper Holdings. She's the one who has pushed for the carriage to be out there.'

'Appreciate it,' said Clarissa, and put the phone down. She got a call back from her contact in Coventry. He said that a lot of the carriages had resided at one time with a Mr Davitt. Apparently, he couldn't be traced anymore.

'Why not?' asked Clarissa.

'The items were sold on, but they were done privately. Mr Davitt was distraught at the death of his wife. The items were sold not long after that, though there's no public receipts. They were then picked up separately as best I know, one by Mr Garrick, though he didn't say where he got it from, and also by a Miss Ursula Knight. The rest—I'm not sure where they went.'

'Do you know what the large one looks like?' asked Clarissa.

'Not really, it's the least expensive and—'

'It's the least expensive, but it's the biggest?' queried Clarissa.

'Well, I say least expensive—it's never had a price put on it. In their history, the rest of them have been bought. The larger one seems to have been taken. It's very shadowy, what went on with the carriages. In their history, there have been people murdered to gain control of them. They are old, hundreds of years old, and yet exquisite.'

'So you're telling me I'm struggling—'

'I heard rumours,' said her contact, 'that they had been picked up in Scotland, although nobody's ever got close enough to verify that they are the real thing. There are rumours they're being held by a Lady MacPhail. She apparently has two carriages, although nobody's ever seen them.'

'Well, that's not surprising,' said Clarissa. 'Probably only for private showings. Anyone else?'

'A Katie Grouse. Not sure who she is, but she's listed in several companies, some of them up your way.'

'Okay,' said Clarissa. *So, if Lady MacPhail has two, Katie Grouse has one, Ursula Knight, and Garrick has two, then the large carriage of Isabel McNeice could be the real one,* thought Clarissa.

At least now she knew where to go. Clarissa looked up the numbers to contact the purported owners of the other carriages. At the very least, she could go there and discover whether they were the true owners. It would be wise to advise them of the theft of Mr Garrick's, even if she didn't say who he was.

After spending an hour making contact and finding the offices of Lady Angela MacPhail, Isabel McNeice, and Katie Grouse, Clarissa tried calling Ursula Knight. It took a couple of different phone calls before she was told to wait. Clarissa sat back in her chair, the phone line remaining open, her microphone muted. It was then that Patterson came over to her.

'I've been working hard,' he said, 'but trying to trace Garrick is a nightmare. The man was seen in Vienna two months ago. He's been in Botswana. He's also been to Australia. Within the last six months, there are rumours of sightings of him, but the only places we know he definitely stayed are proper hotels, and even then, brief stays. Some countries he goes to, we've no idea where he stays. I've also looked at his private jet. It seems to travel an awful lot without him as well.'

'So, you think he's visiting places, telling no one?'

'Who knows? Maybe he sends it off to pick him up after he's come from somewhere else. The long and short of it is,

I cannot trace Garrick at all. The last three months, he's not even been recorded on the jet. Not one of the passengers. There's been some other people using it.'

'But that's not unusual, is it?' asked Clarissa. 'I mean, the Chief Constable's obviously spoken to him.'

'No, he didn't,' said Patterson. 'That's not what Laura Silver said. She said that Mr Garrick had got her to contact the Chief Constable. And the Chief Constable jumped even when his secretary called.'

Clarissa sat back, thinking for a moment. 'I've got the team coming up. We'll be joined by them soon. I've found out the contact details of where I think the other carriages are. We're going to have to verify that,' said Clarissa. 'I want to see if this is going to be a job to grab them all. The true value would lie in having them all.

'Effectively, you could actually put each carriage inside of the other, which is why they think it's possible they could also be Russian. You always had the Russian dolls like that. And these carriages are made the same way. But it means the last carriage is huge,' said Clarissa. 'They're said to be quite stunning, all the tales of them, the surrounding gold with the jewels sitting inside.'

'But what's the point of them?' asked Pat. 'You can't exactly go out in them.'

'Well, there may be one on the parade on Christmas Eve.'

'I guess that's something,' said Patterson. 'I mean, even the king used his carriage during the coronation. So that's something, isn't it? But these don't seem to be used for anything. I never got that. Art that just sits there. Doesn't do anything.'

'Art's for your mind, Pats, all right? And you could do with looking at a lot more of it.'

Patterson shook his head. 'Long and short of it, boss, is that Mr Garrick is almost untraceable. I wouldn't mind speaking to him personally, because we could do with knowing if he's got any enemies. People who would want this.'

'Lots of people would want it,' said Clarissa. 'I think we'll go through the others and see if they've got anybody poking around for theirs. That might be the way to go about it. Anyway, I'm waiting to hear from Ursula Knight.'

Just then, the phone line broke open again and Clarissa unmuted the mic. There was a husky voice on the other end, announcing itself.

'Hello, would that be Detective Inspector Clarissa Urquhart?'

'This is she,' said Clarissa. 'Who am I speaking to?'

'Felix Rastrum. I am a representative of Miss Ursula Knight. I'm afraid Miss Knight is unavailable at the moment. She doesn't make many public appearances or talk to many people these days. She values her privacy.'

'Well, I appreciate that. I just wanted to warn her about something. I believe she may be in possession of one of the Cinderella carriages.'

There was silence on the other end. And then there was a cough.

'Something wrong?' asked Clarissa.

'Why do you ask?'

'Because,' said Clarissa, 'another owner, of what I believe to have been the smallest carriage, has reported it stolen.'

'I think we should meet. You see, Miss Knight has had her carriage stolen as well. It's not public knowledge, and I'd thank you for keeping it that way.'

Clarissa could feel the blood pumping in her veins. Both

stolen! She'd need to get to the rest. This could be it—this could be somebody trying to gather the collection.

'Give me an address and I'll be there,' said Clarissa.

'It's in Pitlochry. Where are you—'

'I'm in Inverness. What I'll do is I'll send my sergeant to you. She's coming up that way. In fact, could be with you within the hour.'

Felix Rastrum passed over an address. 'If you tell her to call this number, I'll make myself available. I have got other duties to do, but if she calls, I'll make sure that she's able to have a look at where the item was stolen from.'

Clarissa put the phone down and almost jumped out of her seat, causing Patterson to look up at her.

'What's the matter?' he asked.

'Second one gone,' she said, and grabbed the phone again. 'I'm going to get Sabine and Emmett to get there. Something big's up on this one, Pats. I tell you now, something big.'

Chapter 04

Sabine Ferguson was not that long out of Glasgow, with Emmett in the passenger seat of the car, when the call came through from Clarissa to divert them to Pitlochry. Detective Sergeant Sabine Ferguson had been hoping for a quiet Christmas. Sabine was particularly disappointed because that night she was going to attend the board game group that Detective Sergeant Emmett Grump belonged to. She'd been going along for several weeks now, enjoying the friendliness of it.

Sabine had been more used to groups that had been doing workouts—Pilates—and although she wasn't getting to them as often, she still enjoyed those groups. She was finding in Emmett a friend whom she could talk to. Sabine wasn't used to having a male friend who wasn't interested in her romantically. Yes, there were occasional men in her work-out groups, but she didn't chat with them that much. They certainly weren't close friends.

Emmett, however, seemed to want nothing except a chat and a companion to play his board games with. What was quite funny was how certain people at the station were now tagging them as a couple, when in fact it was the last thing on their minds. They just played board games together.

Emmett was also learning from Sabine, taking on board the different art books, videos, and programs that Sabine had recommended for his education in the arts world. He was studious. She gave him that, taking free moments at work to be buried in a book or watching an online video. But now they'd been dragged away from their evening, and with a trip to Inverness, she knew she would not get back quickly. However, they packed and got going as quickly as they could. Now it seemed they were going to work on the way up.

Pitlochry, like most of the north of Scotland, was covered in snow. The A9 had remained quite good because of the snow ploughing that had cleared it. But as they got off the road towards Pitlochry, some roads were less well maintained. It was only normal—the main roads got all the excellent treatment, and gradually the snow ploughs would work out to the minor roads.

But some of the smaller roads were difficult to maintain, with their twists and their curves, and there was a skimming of snow underneath. Not enough cars passed that way to break the snow down, and the air was so cold. Glasgow had hit minus nine the night before. It hadn't snowed, probably too cold to snow, but the snow that was there wasn't going away.

'Where's this house?' Sabine asked Emmett.

'Sat nav says round the next corner, take a left, and then we should see it.'

Sabine followed the road, and sure enough, they approached a house. It wasn't large, but it was modern, and it was set back on its own grounds. As they approached the large metal gate, Sabine parked the car, and Emmett got out and walked over to a panel in a pillar beside the gate. He pressed the intercom switch.

'Hello?' asked a voice.

'Hello! It's Detective Sergeant Emmett Grump, along with Detective Sergeant Sabine Ferguson. We are here to investigate the theft that you reported.'

'Come in,' said the voice quickly.

The gate rolled to one side as Emmett got back into the car. Sabine drove up the driveway and parked in front of the house. There was presumably a full lawn somewhere under the snow, and the house was surrounded by trees beyond that buried lawn. It was secluded to a point, but the modern build of it made it stand out from the gate.

The front door opened as they got out of the car, and a smallish man stood there. He had a petite frame with black and scruffy hair, barely reaching down to his neck. It was hard to place his age. Maybe thirty? He dressed all in black: black trousers, black jacket, with a black shirt underneath. The jacket was smartly done across, buttoned up, even though his hands were in his pockets. He had black shoes on that were immaculate, too.

'Hello there,' said Sabine. 'I'm Detective Sergeant Sabine Ferguson, my colleague, DS Emmett Grump. Who would you be?'

'My name is Felix Rastrum. I spoke to Detective Inspector Urquhart. My boss, Ursula Knight, is regrettably not here at the moment. She travels quite a bit with her work. I hope you understand. She has left instructions I am to accommodate you as best as possible.'

Sabine looked closely at the man and actually wondered: was it a man? He was one of those androgynous people. Quite feminine in a lot of ways, and yet she could have sworn he could be a man as well. In the right clothing, she wouldn't have a clue. Emmett, however, didn't stop to look, but strolled forward to shake hands.

'If you'd be so kind as to show us where, when, and what happened, that would be most appreciated,' said Emmett.

He walked up to the front door of the house and kicked his boots against the wall, dropping snow off them. Sabine followed suit but noticed that Felix didn't bother, even though there was snow on his shoes after stepping beyond the door's threshold.

'It's quite bemusing,' said Felix, 'and I think it must have been done by somebody very professional. The thing is, we have the height of security here: locks, codes, number pads. You can't get into here without knowing them. Infrared, fingerprints, the lot. I wasn't here when it was stolen. Nobody was, but if you come and have a look at our video room, you'll see that, well, they've wiped the time when it was taken.'

Sabine followed Felix into a small room with a large screen. While Emmett and she stood behind the man, he ran through the video footage. It showed an empty house and nothing moving. In a time gap of approximately forty minutes after that, the house resumed to its normal state, except that a small carriage that had been in the living room was gone.

'Can you take me to that room?' said Sabine.

'Of course,' said Felix. His voice wasn't quite gruff, and Sabine felt it should have been deeper; it was more like a teenager's, reaching high pitches at times. Squeaky.

She followed the man through and came to a well-laid-out living room with all modern conveniences. There were several items sitting around, and Felix pointed to a particular spot on a table.

'That's where the carriage would have sat.'

'And how big was the carriage?' asked Sabine.

The man indicated something that was around about the size of Sabine's hand times three.

'Do you know of the carriages?' asked Felix.

'Like most people, I've never actually seen them, but I know the stories, the tales.'

'This is the second one. Well, the second smallest.'

'How did Miss Knight acquire it?' asked Emmett.

'That's not something my employer shared with me,' said Felix. 'I believe it was legitimate though, if private.'

'Who was the seller?'

'Again, unfortunately not something that my employer has asked me to share with you. Or that she's shared with me. She's also asked that none of her security measures are discussed. So, beyond the footage and showing you what I believe we've been hacked into, I'm not at liberty to go any further.'

'That will severely hinder our investigation,' said Sabine. 'You are aware of that?'

'I've got to be honest with you,' said Felix. 'My employer is doing this more as a courtesy. Your detective inspector called. I was under instruction that if any police were to approach us, that I would inform you of the loss of the carriage, but I wasn't to inform them directly. She's also said that I may show you what happened, but not to give you any detail of our own personal security. We have a lot of other items.'

'Can I ask something?' said Emmett, still staring around the room, not particularly at any item. 'Is there much in here of value?'

'No, no,' said Felix, 'although that would depend on your

idea of money.'

'Items the same price as the carriage,' said Emmett.

'It was probably the most expensive item in here.'

'Why is it in here?' asked Emmett. 'As far as I am aware, most private collectors, if they have something of significant value, have a strong room. They'd at least have a room where they can enjoy their items, but which is particularly protected. This seems to be one of the most open rooms you have.'

'Miss Knight particularly liked the carriage, and she liked it in front of her. This is her most comfortable room, where she spends her time when she is here.'

'Where is she at the moment?' asked Sabine.

'About business. Again, she doesn't tell me everything.'

'What's she looking from us for this investigation?' asked Sabine.

'She's not,' said Felix. 'She'll have her own methods of trying to find things out, I assume. And she'll go about it that way. She said this was as a courtesy because you may know more about the other carriages. She doesn't. Yes, she knows of certain ones and their locations, but she doesn't know the owners. I'm sure she'd be looking into them now. Certainly, I would.'

'Because?'

'Because, DS Grump, it's one of a set. And collectors, I've always found, when they get one of a set, want to get the rest of the set. Don't you think?'

'I guess so,' said Emmett. 'I just bought the last of a series of board games. They all go together. I guess it's a bit like that. Probably more expensive, though. Although, the board and card games are getting expensive these days,' said Emmett, staring off into another corner of the room. 'Regretfully so. They've got superb pictures in them.'

'Indeed,' said Felix. 'I don't mean to rush you, but is there anything else I can help you with?'

'Would you mind if I take any photographs?' asked Sabine.

'My boss has asked that you don't,' said Felix. 'But you have my number, and by all means, please call. I will be available, but if you call ahead, it means that I won't be out. I do have other tasks that Miss Knight asked me to do. This isn't the only residence I look after for her.'

'Where are the rest of them?' asked Emmett.

'About Scotland.'

'Would you like to tell me where?' said Emmett.

'Miss Knight doesn't like to give away her private retreats.'

'She's quite shadowy, isn't she?' said Emmett.

'She likes to protect her privacy,' said Felix. 'That's all. I hope that by engaging with you, we're showing that we're not anti what you would do, and we're not actually a part of this. Apparently, another carriage went missing.'

'Well, thank you,' said Sabine. 'I think I've got enough. I'm not sure what we can do for your boss, but we'll keep you informed of our investigations and, by all means, we will contact you if we need you again.'

'That's very kind,' said Felix, although Sabine didn't feel that he thought that at all.

They were shown to the door and Felix watched them as they got into the car and drove to the gate, which opened for them. Once back on the road, Sabine found a coffee shop in Pitlochry, and they sat down together to discuss what they'd seen.

'Slightly cavalier attitude, don't you think? I think some of my board games are better protected.'

'They do have some security, though,' said Sabine.

'Yes,' said Emmett, 'security that seems to have been breached rather easily, and then had video footage destroyed.'

'Without getting into the systems, it's going to be very hard to verify how that was done or why it was done. Or indeed, if anything could have been recovered.'

'Exactly,' said Emmett. 'That troubles me. If that's your favourite item, and you're not there often, why would you leave it?'

'It's the old thing though,' said Sabine. 'If you're going to hide something, hide it in the open.'

'How can you hide something like that?' said Emmett. 'Surely people would know what it is.'

'Not a lot,' said Sabine. 'You'd have to know what you were looking for. You'd have to get into the house, first of all. One would have to assume there's a security system that would prevent you from getting into the house.'

'As you said,' said Emmett, 'we don't know. She's not exactly been forthcoming. And that Felix guy. Something's bugging me about him.'

'We can't complain. He told us what we needed to know.'

'Yes,' said Emmett, but he seemed unconvinced. The pair finished their coffees and got back on the road.

Back in the car, they began making their way up the road, with the mountains on either side covered in snow. Sabine enjoyed the drive, but Emmett was looking agitated.

'Why now?' said Emmett.

'What do you mean?' asked Sabine.

'That's one of her favourite places. That's why the item is there. Why would you be stealing it now?'

'Most likely for it to be around over Christmas.'

'They're still doing business up to this time. They could

be at balls, dinners, something somewhere else. There's no guarantee of that.'

Emmett gave a sigh and then turned and started looking out of the window at the whiteness that raced past. Here in the mountains, snow was falling.

Sabine tried to focus as that tunnel of flakes came towards the car. They would be a good couple of hours up the road and darkness was beginning to fall.

Chapter 05

'Well, it's about time you two got here.'

Sabine walked on into the office, but Emmett stood for a moment in the doorway, staring at Clarissa.

'If you hadn't sent us off to Pitlochry, we'd have been up here in good time,' said Emmett.

'What she means,' said Sabine, 'is couldn't you have put the foot down more in the car? But I couldn't. I drive safely. I don't hurtle around in that green machine.'

'And you could have left the attitude down in Glasgow as well,' said Clarissa.

'Attitude's what you pay me for,' said Sabine, and plonked herself down in the spare chair across from Patterson's desk. 'How are we doing, Eric?'

'You're looking well,' said Patterson. 'Really bubbly.'

'It's not compliments' time. It's time to get to work,' said Clarissa.

'I thought we were touching base to then go off to the hotel,' said Sabine.

'We'll see. We need to pull together what we've got first,' said Clarissa. 'Emmett, grab a seat. You're making the doorway look untidy.'

Emmett gave her a scowl before walking over and placing himself on the edge of her desk. 'I'm good to go,' he said.

Clarissa stared at him. She wasn't sure about Emmett yet. Well, he was a good detective. Very good, according to Macleod, for whom he'd done some work recently. But she wasn't sure how to play him. Sabine rolled off her brashness. Emmett almost seemed to have a dislike of it. Strange.

'Can I get a coffee first?' said Sabine.

'Hasn't Pats got a flask ready yet?' said Clarissa.

Patterson shook his head as he stood up but Emmett put his hand up. 'I'll get them,' he said.

'It's fine,' said Patterson.

'This is your sergeant talking. No, it's not. Sit down.' Emmett jumped off the table and made his way out of the office, heading for the kitchen area.

'Did you jump at this?' said Sabine, looking over at Clarissa who glared back at her.

'Jump at what?' said Clarissa.

'Cinderella carriages. It's right up your street, isn't it?'

It was, and Clarissa had jumped at it, but there was no way she was going to admit that. 'I took a rather unfavourable request to come in during my Christmas time off,' said Clarissa.

'She left Frank sitting there, half-eaten mince pie, and disappeared out the door before the poor man could even say goodbye.'

Clarissa glared up at the doorway where Macleod was now standing.

'I'm about to brief the team. What are you wanting?' she said in a deliberately impertinent tone.

'Excellent,' said Macleod. 'I'm here to provide my wisdom,

and to hear what's going on.'

'We're on top of this,' she said. 'It's not a problem.'

'And it's not a problem for me either. Jane's not expecting me for another half an hour, so, I can take in your wisdom. Paperwork's done for the day.'

Macleod walked over and sat down on the edge of Clarissa's desk, right where Emmett had. It made Clarissa think. Did they know how to wind her up? Was this deliberate?

'You better tell Emmett you want one,' Clarissa said to Macleod.

Macleod simply sat there with a slightly smug grin on his face. A minute later, Emmett walked in and placed a coffee in front of Macleod.

'I think that's how you like it,' said Emmett.

'Where's mine?' said Clarissa.

'Just bringing the DCI's through first,' said Emmett. He disappeared back out and then came in with a tray with the rest of them. Sabine smiled from the far corner, and Clarissa wondered was the whole joke on her.

'Right,' she said, 'let's get on to this.'

She flicked on a small screen on the wall which her laptop connected up to, pressing the start of a PowerPoint show. She put an image up on the wall. 'A rather old image of Mr Garrick, who had his property stolen from a rather demure estate in the Cairngorms. Not heavily protected and had only one member of staff there, a Laura Silver. Mr Garrick's movements are very hard to trace.

'Pats had a go and can't get near him. Very reclusive man but owned one of the Cinderella carriages. These items, for those who don't know,' she said pointedly, glaring at Macleod, 'almost have cult status. They have been hard to follow but are now owned by private collectors. They have kept their heads down, which is incredible considering that there are six carriages, each larger than the previous one, and ending up in one that is a full-size carriage.

'All of the carriages can be placed inside one another, but they have not been in the same group for quite a while as far as we understand. The whole batch was sold on privately some time ago to different parties. I've located these parties, but I am not getting information on where they got the carriages from. We'll certainly not get much from Mr Garrick.'

'Can't you force it out of them? Employ a bit of pressure?' asked Macleod.

'Not with somebody like Garrick. Ursula Knight owned the second one that got stolen from Pitlochry.' Macleod raised his eyebrows at that. 'I only just had the team pass through,' said Clarissa. 'We're looking for the update from our Glasgow two.'

'Well, we went in,' said Sabine. 'Ursula Knight's not there either. Again, some of her movements are not the easiest to track. She has many places and is always on the move.'

'Are these dodgy dealers or something?' asked Macleod.

'They're private collectors, Seoras, and people who value their anonymity. These people have serious money.'

'But the paparazzi will not follow them around, will they? I mean, why? Why so secretive?'

'They are. They just are, Okay?' said Clarissa. 'And they don't advertise what they've got. One of the key things about private collections is that they're private. People are apoplectic to have the artwork themselves. They don't want it on show; they will not tell everyone about it. They have it; the ownership is the joy; having it with them is the joy—not telling everyone "look at me."'

'Continue,' Macleod said to Sabine.

'It's a very modern house the second carriage was taken from, but it was placed in a living room that had little to protect it. The house itself had very modern security systems, but whoever came in got past them and erased about forty minutes of tape so they weren't seen taking the item. Quite frankly, there's nothing there. They won't let us go in with a team. They're looking after their own security, and it's basically been passed on to us as a courtesy because you phoned to tell them about the other carriage,' said Sabine, nodding at Clarissa.

'So, hang on for a minute,' said Macleod. 'They don't want any help to recover this. Are they bringing third parties in?'

'Definitely,' said Clarissa. 'I would fully expect that.'

'Would you recognise the third party?'

'Probably. So would Sabine. Pats and Emmett would struggle.'

Macleod simply nodded, then awaited the conversation to continue.

'That's two carriages been taken, the smallest ones. There are bigger carriages out there and I've traced the owners, I think,' said Clarissa. 'What we need to do is contact these owners and warn them, and then keep an eye. One of the carriages, I believe, is going to be used in the Christmas parade in Inverness on Christmas Eve. It's a full-size carriage, and I'm struggling to see how they're going to nick it.'

'What's the set worth together?' asked Emmett.

'Priceless. Some of this stuff is priceless. It's never been sold like that before. We don't know what anybody bought it for the last time. You don't put a figure on this.'

'Mr Garrick did,' said Macleod.

'Mr Garrick and Miss Knight didn't tell anyone. Didn't even tell anyone they had it. That's the whole point,' said Clarissa. 'These things are not going to . . . to be easy to deal with.'

'So what are we looking at?' asked Sabine.

'Well, two of the next-two-sized carriages up are actually owned by the same person,' said Clarissa. 'It's a Lady Angela Macphail, Lord Macphail's wife. Don't know if anybody knows her.'

'Seen her in some publications. She's a well-built, large lady,' said Emmett.

Clarissa nodded. 'Anything else about her?'

'Well, I think she could show off to her friends. I didn't see any carriages though when she was in the *Country Living*.'

'Tread carefully,' said Macleod. 'I don't want people getting too upset. We're there to help. I don't want Lord MacPhail coming in to complain. The Chief Constable is the one who instigated this investigation. He will not be happy if it comes back that we're annoying people, especially people in his circle.'

'That's not like you,' said Clarissa. 'You're the sort of person who would just barge through the circles.'

'Not when there's no need to barge,' said Macleod. 'At the moment, I've got some things on the go I want the Chief Constable to help me with and to agree to. Okay? Softly, softly,' said Macleod.

'We always go softly in the arts team.'

Macleod glared over at Clarissa. 'Bull in a china shop, more like,' he said.

'Well, if I can get on then,' said Clarissa, 'the second largest of the carriages is owned by a Katie Grouse.'

'She's a rather successful businesswoman,' said Patterson. 'A lot of money behind her, a lot of clout. Everything seems legit though.'

'She's a collector. We're not talking criminals here,' said Clarissa.

'Well, not yet,' said Sabine. Clarissa glared over at her.

'Got a hold of her secretary to get some timings to see her. The last one was owned by Isabel McNeice. She's from Hamper Holdings. Hamper Holdings, of course, busy time . . . they're getting their last hampers out for Christmas—their sales come through and they deliver them this last week. They're also involved in the Christmas parade, so she's a very busy woman, and we're going to see her as well. She has the largest carriage though. It will be kept properly, I would suspect.'

'So the plan's what? Tell these people the other two have been nicked and read their faces?' said Macleod.

'Basically, yes, Seoras,' said Clarissa. 'We can't trace Garrick; we can't trace Knight. They won't let us in to assess properly the area where it's been stolen. Frankly, from a police perspective, why are we interested? Things have been stolen, but the owners don't really want us involved.'

'Except that Mr Garrick wants you involved. He specifically asked our Chief Constable to get you involved.'

'And yet he won't let me go into the house, check through it, bring forensics in. Wants to keep his own security. Doesn't want to bring attention to himself.'

'I agree,' said Macleod. 'It's a little strange.'

'It's more than a little,' said Emmett. 'Can we force his hand? Can we say to him—'

'Didn't get that impression,' said Patterson.

'Are we talking a high-tech team here,' asked Macleod, 'to break in and grab this stuff?'

'Somebody needs to know about all the alarms on the

Pitlochry site,' said Emmett.

'You could have walked in off the road and grabbed it up in the Cairngorms,' said Patterson.

'That being said,' said Sabine, 'the other one was in the living room as well, in Pitlochry. It was one of the easiest rooms to get into. We didn't see a safe room, but if you've got a lot of artwork, you keep them in a protected room, generally.'

'So why were they out?'

'Well, sure, Garrick just likes to have somewhere that people don't know about. His anonymity worked. I would suspect he's probably anxious,' said Clarissa, 'at the moment. More worried about his actual loss of anonymity than his loss of the carriage.'

'And in Pitlochry. Strange,' says Sabine. 'It's not protected. Could you get in past the systems? Probably, and if you do, you walk in, you grab it, you walk out and reset them. There's no major problem if you can get past those initial defences, which a very high-tech team could. We are talking about expensive stuff. This isn't anything bargain basement.'

'Basically,' said Clarissa, 'we have got nothing. So we're all going to go out and we're going to shake the tree. Sabine, I want you to see Grouse. The lady's a professional woman. You look the part for that. Emmett, seeing as you're very well versed with our Lady McPhail, why don't you go and talk to her? See what you can dig up. Myself and Patterson are off to see Isabel McNeice tomorrow.'

'Good,' said Macleod. 'I suggest you all go home and get a good night's sleep. Maybe you can crack this by Christmas,' said Macleod to Clarissa.

'We'd better crack it before Christmas. Last year we were running around an Inverness parade, up on a stage stopping a lunatic. I want to spend Christmas Eve in front of a telly with Frank,' she said.

'Oh, by the way,' said Macleod, 'I kept him company. Had one of those mince pies with brandy sauce. He's spot on about that.'

Clarissa didn't rise to the bait as Macleod stood up off the edge of the table and drained his coffee. As he left, going out the door, he turned and said, 'Don't worry if we have to work through Christmas. Frank can always come to us for dinner.'

Macleod had left the door entrance when the pen came whizzing through the open door and hit the wall on the far side of the corridor.

'I'm going to kill that man one day,' said Clarissa out loud.

'Are we good to go?' asked Sabine. 'I've still got a hotel to get into.'

'First thing in the morning, though, get on and get these people interviewed. There's a sheet of paper on the corner of my desk. It's got the contact numbers. Let's see if we can dig out where our next target is because I think this is a serial collector. Somebody who wants the lot.'

Emmett got up to go after Patterson said he'd wash the cups. As he passed Clarissa's desk, she put her hand out to stop him.

'Sergeant Grump,' said Clarissa. 'Next time, you make my coffee with Seoras's—'

'Just keeping the DCI sweet for you,' said Emmett. 'He is, after all, the big boss.' Emmett's face was completely straight when he said it, but Sabine burst out laughing behind him.

'Get out,' said Clarissa. 'We'll turn the tables on Seoras before Christmas Day.'

Chapter 06

Sabine Ferguson brushed her hair in the hotel's mirror. It was one of those standard hotels that were up and down the country, but you always knew what you were getting. It wasn't cheap at this time of the year, but it was warm, and with the cold air outside, Sabine was glad of that.

Emmett was in a room just down the corridor from her, and they'd spent about half an hour last night talking through some rules of one of his board games. Sabine had been having trouble with it, but Emmett was explaining it to her, and she found herself becoming incredibly caught up in his made-up world.

Sabine had dug out of her suitcase what she thought would be appropriate today. The way Clarissa had talked, she'd thought about putting on a long, narrow skirt, looking the business type of woman. But to be honest, it was so cold, there was no way she was doing that. So, she put on her black jeans, long black boots, a light brown scarf around her neck, and a large jacket. She finished it with a fedora, just for that slightly classy look. It was funny, Sabine thought. She never would have worn this going elsewhere, but since she'd met Emmett, he'd encouraged her to be the character in their gaming that she wanted to be in real life.

Sabine knew she looked good. She had a decent figure. She could dress the part. But she didn't want to dress the way the magazines said. 'How to power dress for work and business.' She preferred those adventure characters. That's who she wanted to be, and that was why the fedora was going on top. She was off on her own today and if it didn't work, she could always put it away again.

She looked in the mirror and grinned before making her way down to breakfast. Breakfast had to be a quick affair because she had to get on the road, and she saw Emmett while she was eating. He clocked the hat sitting beside her seat, and told her to put it on. He grinned when she did.

'That's you,' he said. 'That's definitely you.' Sabine had to run quickly after that to get to her early morning appointment.

Katie Grouse's people had said she had a breakfast meeting, but that Sabine could catch her at the house before she left after it. Sabine drove the car out to the outskirts of Inverness, and when she pulled up at the house, she almost collapsed. It was so large and breathtaking. It was like it said to you, 'You don't have a house. You just have a little sty. This is a house done properly.'

There was class everywhere, too. The place was stylish, yet incredibly functional. As she approached the front door, which was opened by a maid, Ferguson admired some of the modern architecture. Sure, she normally dealt with older stuff, but she could admire the new too. She was led through by the maid to wait on a chair in a hallway.

Ferguson could see out of the rear of the house and saw an enormous garden, currently covered in white but which had a river flowing through. She stood up and walked over to the windows, absolutely flabbergasted at the grounds behind the house.

'I'm sure Maria told you to wait in the chair.'

'Just rather taken by the view,' said Sabine, turning around.

In front of her was a woman who, while not obese in any way, was a rather large lady. Her shoulders were stacked, and her general figure started out wide and came in towards her feet. She wore a suit with a blouse underneath, her brown hair parted just left of middle and descending to her ears. It looked stylish, but incredibly practical. Her suit was creased slightly; it gave the appearance that it was a working outfit, not one for going out in. Her shoes, too, were sandals. No high heels, nothing to try to say, 'Look at me.' Instead, she appeared all business.

'I'm Detective Sergeant Sabine Ferguson from the Arts Division. I believe my inspector called you.'

'Your Inspector got hold of my people. I'm Katie Grouse.'

'Pleasure to meet you, Miss Grouse,' said Sabine, pulling a warrant card out from within her jacket. Katie Grouse took it and examined it almost minutely before handing it back. 'I believe you to be the owner of one of the Cinderella carriages,' said Sabine.

'That's correct,' said Grouse. 'You've done well to trace them down. Few people know their whereabouts, although I don't keep it a particular secret.'

'You don't advertise either, though.'

'Well, why should I? I don't want anybody else to come and look at it.'

'Which carriage is it?' asked Sabine, looking for clarification.

'It's the penultimate one,' said Katie. 'It is large, but I enjoy it.'

'You don't seem like an art collector.'

'Sometimes the meaning is in the object,' said Katie. 'I won't profess to being a particular collector of art. I have some artwork, as an investment. The carriage is not just an investment. It says something else to me.'

'And what is that?' asked Sabine.

'Well, that's quite personal,' said Katie. 'You have some information for me, though?'

'I regret to inform you that the smallest two of the Cinderella carriages have been stolen. And I'm here to advise you to keep a close eye on your own, and also to advise us if anyone approaches you looking to sell or looking for information on the carriages.'

'Well, that's noted,' said Katie. She turned away.

'Can I ask where you acquired the carriage?'

Grouse stopped. 'I have a business meeting to get to.'

'So I was told,' said Sabine. 'Again, could I ask where you acquired the carriage?'

'I bought it in a secret auction, but I have the paperwork for it.'

'Can I see that?'

Katie Grouse turned and stared at Sabine. 'If you must, sergeant,' she said.

There was a click of the fingers and a young lady ran up to her. 'Go and get the paperwork for the carriage. The sergeant needs to see it, okay?' The woman nodded her head and shot off. Katie turned back towards Sabine. 'Do you know much about the art world, or are you just a plod?'

'I know plenty,' said Sabine.

'Good. I'd hate to think they sent some idiot out. I was half expecting that Urquhart woman. Seen her at some auctions.'

'Detective Inspector Urquhart's my boss,' said Sabine. 'And she knows her stuff.'

'I'm aware of that,' said Katie.

The paperwork arrived quickly after that, and Katie held it in front of her. It all looked okay. It had been a secret auction, and the seller's name was there: Oliver Davitt.

'Would you say how much he sold it to you for?'

'No, I wouldn't,' said Katie. 'We don't wish people to be putting prices on such an item.'

'Oliver Davitt, did he own many of them?'

'I think he owned them all at one point,' said Katie.

'So how did you get into that auction?'

'Would your inspector ask that question? It's a secret auction. There are ways and means. Sometimes you have to scratch a few backs, just to be in the room, just to get a chance to make a bid. That's all I'm telling you.'

'You have other items, though,' she said.

'I do.'

'Could I see those? And the carriage, of course.'

'If you must,' said Katie. 'As quick as we can, though, please. I have a meeting to get on to.'

Katie Grouse strolled through the house until she appeared at a metal door with a keypad outside. She punched in a 12-digit code without blinking or hesitating. The door opened. She stepped inside with Sabine, and once inside, Sabine could see that the woman was indeed a collector.

There were paintings, sculptures, and bits of woodwork that Sabine recognised as being worth considerable sums of money. She looked around at some protections on the displays, each item secured differently to the one before.

'I see you take your security very seriously. That's good, but where's the carriage?'

'This room is too small for the carriage. The carriage has its own place.'

Sabine was escorted back out of the room, down several more halls, until she arrived in a conservatory. There on the floor sat the carriage. It wasn't quite up to Sabine's waist, but it wasn't far off it. You could fit a doll into it, a good-sized doll. Sabine bent down beside it, staring at the fixtures, looking here and there around it. It certainly looked to be genuine.

'Why is it here?' asked Sabine.

'I told you, it's too big for the other room. Wouldn't have fitted in correctly. And besides, I like it.'

Sabine stood looking at the carriage, and then out the windows of the conservatory, onto that fantastically white lawn.

'It goes nowhere else?' asked Sabine.

'No, I haven't wanted to take it anywhere. It has a sentimental value to me more than a monetary value, so I like it where I can see it. I sometimes sit in the conservatory. I also have a piano over there in the corner that I play. It's nice to look across and see the carriage. I had this mount made for it so it could sit up at a nice height. It's a great thing to view when you've had a tiring day.'

'I'm sure it is,' said Sabine.

'If you're quite finished—'

'I think so. Like I said, this is just a warning that some of the other carriages have been taken. So, I hope it might cause you to put a little extra security on at the moment.'

'No one has ever been in this house without being asked in,' said Katie. 'I appreciate your time,' she said, obviously not appreciating it, 'but I know how to look after my gear. Kindly tell your inspector not to worry, and if I see anyone or anything coming for my carriage, I will advise her. Good day to you.'

She turned on her heel and walked out of the room. Almost instantly, the young lady who had retrieved the paperwork appeared, indicating that Sabine should make for the front door.

As Sabine got out and sat in her car, she looked around. Something didn't sit with her. All of these items were just so randomly left, and although Katie Grouse said that the carriage was too big, it wasn't. She could have fitted it in the safe room with a bit of rearrangement. She could have got somebody to do that; it wasn't as if she couldn't afford help.

Something wasn't right. She'd meet up with Emmett once he was done with his interview and compare notes. For now, Sabine was having trouble that such expensive items, almost mythological items in terms of where they'd been, were just being placed here and there willy nilly. Were they being stolen to get an insurance claim? How much could they be insured for? Who would insure it? An enormous payout on something that was beyond price.

Sabine sighed and drove the car out of the driveway. So far, in this case, nobody seemed to want their help. *Well, let's hope they don't need it*, thought Sabine. She went to head back towards the office, but stopped off for a pasty and a cup of coffee. The air was frosty, but as she stood looking out over part of the Moray Firth, she smiled.

It was different to Glasgow up here, wasn't it? It really was the Highlands. Big city in Glasgow. In some ways, she liked it, but this would be a good place to come up to, she thought. Not that she'd get a transfer. They liked the art team spread out, and Clarissa was top dog, so she'd be where she wanted to be. Spread the rest of the team out elsewhere.

So, Sabine sucked in the sea air and breathed out. The Clyde was different, very different from here. But how would she get here? She smiled to herself. One day she would. One day.

Chapter 07

DS Emmett Grump picked up a pool car from the station and drove his way out to visit Lady Angela MacPhail. Emmett was dressed in black trousers, a white shirt that had no tie, and a rain jacket. He wasn't really for being that smart, and now being away from home, he had travelled with little of a wardrobe. There was a tie available, but he'd chosen not to wear it because he hated them; anything around the neck bothered Emmett. As he drove through Inverness, along the river, he looked at the houses passing by. He was just outside the city, not towards the new estates, but an older run of road where the Loch Ness Marathon ran past.

Finding the house wasn't difficult, given the look of it. Emmett enjoyed medieval things. He was quite happy if his gaming evenings turned into something about dwarfs, elves, and men with enormous castles. There were swords, clubs, shields, plate armour, and women in long, flowing gowns. It was all a bit of a laugh, really, wasn't it?

But as he stopped before the house of Lady Angela MacPhail, he had a feeling that someone had gone too far. The building was castle-like and had turrets along the top, and yet it was modern. It did everything not to blend into the fairy tale it was trying to create; instead, it looked like the plastic castle you'd find at a children's amusement park.

He parked his car outside the gate and strolled along to find an intercom. After gaining admittance, he wandered up the driveway and stood outside the front door until it was slowly opened by an elderly gentleman.

'DS Emmett Grump. I have an appointment with her ladyship,' said Emmett, trying to keep to the formalities. Emmett wasn't one for being aggressive with people; he liked to disarm them by putting them at an ease so they said things that they probably shouldn't. So, with someone who was a lady, he would keep the formality, let her think she was in charge.

'Her ladyship is ready for you in the drawing room,' said the older man. He had immaculate trousers on with a waistcoat and even gloves on his hands. Emmett dutifully followed him as he was led through several corridors with many portraits on every wall. Emmett did not know if any of them were expensive, and he thought that some of them looked like they may be family portraits.

The older man opened the door and swept into a room with a chaise longue on the far side. There were a couple of other chairs sitting around—the expensive, well-made kind— as well as a wall full of books, and he wondered if they had ever been touched. He turned and faced the chaise longue where a woman was standing up.

Although it was early in the morning, barely past nine o'clock, she was dressed in a long flowing gown that reminded Emmett of some of his nights role-playing in a medieval era. She was a large woman, not wholly unattractive, but she dwarfed Emmett, not with height but in the voluminous size of her. She had long blonde hair that rolled in waves down past her shoulders, with a face that most probably wouldn't have looked twice at except for the penetrating eyes.

'Detective Sergeant Emmett Grump,' said the older man. He gave a swift bow and made his way out. Emmett wasn't completely sure how to behave to a ladyship, but he stood almost at attention and gave a smile.

'Detective Sergeant,' said the woman in a rather high voice.

'Your ladyship,' said Emmett.

'Always happy to welcome one of the constabulary to my humble abode. How are you this day?'

'I'm okay,' said Emmett, wondering if the voice was real or not. It spoke with a haughtiness that Emmett felt was forced.

'Well, man, tell me why it is you're here. What disturbs me at this hour?'

'Apologies for the interruption,' said Emmett. 'I believe you may be the owner of two of the Cinderella carriages. Would I be correct in that assumption?'

'You are! Exquisite pieces.'

'I regret to inform you that two of the sister carriages, the smallest carriages, have been stolen. I'm here to give you a warning about that. Also to see if you've noticed anything unusual around your premises, or near your carriages, or if you've been approached.'

'How frightful,' said the woman. 'Stolen? From whom?'

Emmett gave her a smile. 'The two collectors,' he said. 'And what's bothering us is that they were very private people. People who didn't flaunt that they had the carriages. We feel that somebody may be making a bid to obtain all six of them.'

'Well, in that case,' said the woman, turning. She walked

over to the wall at the side. A little cord hung down; she pulled it, and Emmett could hear a clanging in the building. *Surely when they built it new, they'd have put in a better system than that,* thought Emmett. *Maybe she wanted it; it was so bizarre.*

'I'll get Magnus. Magnus is my security man; he can advise you.'

'Can I ask something?'

'Of course,' said Lady Angela.

'Would you tell me how you came to be in ownership of the carriages?'

'It was a secret auction. I have the paperwork.'

'And where do you keep them?' asked Emmett.

'A moment. Magnus will show you where, talk to you about everything. They've been here for months except that, well, tomorrow evening they'll be being moved. They're not that large, obviously; the bigger one takes at least two people to shift it, but one of my friends is running a little do. A charity gig, very exclusive people, so we'll be popping them round to that just so people have something to see. She doesn't have quality items, looking to do her best, but, well, sometimes you have to bring a bit of class along, don't you?'

Emmett didn't bat an eyelid but instead, glancing around the room, he thought, *I don't think I can say this out loud, but there's a fakeness about it all. It isn't just an attempt to be something you aren't.* He turned back to Lady Angela. 'I take it your husband paid for the carriages when you got them?'

'Oh no,' said Lady Angela, almost affronted. 'I obtained them long before I met Georgie. Like I say, it was a secret auction. An exclusive number of people along. And I used my family inheritance to acquire them. They were paid with cash, but I did get a receipt. It shows ownership. The person selling it on didn't want to be identified. It happens a lot in this field, the antique world and that. It's rather shadowy, isn't it? In some ways, it's rather fun.'

'I can see how you would think that,' said Emmett, almost upsetting her. 'May I ask, were there any other carriages sold at this auction?'

'Yes,' said Lady Angela, rather hesitantly.

'You didn't think about picking up more of the collection?'

'Well, no,' she said. 'Matter of finance. I may look like I'm full of money at the moment, but back then—while I had some money and a good family inheritance—I wasn't yet fully into the station of life that I deserved. One that Georgie has brought me into.'

Emmett heard the door open behind him.

'Magnus,' said Lady Angela, sweeping across the floor to stand beside a rather diminutive man. He wore a dark grey suit and gave a rather laboured smile towards Lady Angela.

'This is Magnus, my head of security. He'll take you round everything.'

'Well, that's most kind,' said Emmett. 'One last thing before he does that. Will you be leaving the country? It's just that we want to contact you if necessary. Update you in case anything else happens to the other pieces.'

'Most kind,' said Lady Angela. 'But no, we're not off to the sun for at least three months. I do need my constitutional every now and again. A couple of weeks away. It's the trouble with Scotland, isn't it? When the sun shines, it's perfect. Not so much when it doesn't.'

'Proper dreich at times,' said Emmett, and noticed how she almost jumped back from his rather local use of language.

'Well, absolutely. I'll take your warning on board, of course.

Talk more to Magnus,' said Lady Angela. 'And hopefully, I won't have to see you again. I don't mean that in a bad way but, hopefully, you can find whoever took the other carriages and return them to their rightful owners. Magnus here will keep ours safe, no doubt. Very well, thank you for your time, Detective Sergeant.'

Emmett almost bowed before leaving, but instead, he raised his hand up to his head, as if doffing a flat cap. Lady Angela seemed pleased with it, although Emmett was almost confused by his own actions. Magnus led him out of the drawing room, closed the door, and then turned to him.

'My name is Magnus,' he said, 'and I am the head of security. However, I'm the head of security for all of Lord MacPhail's businesses and premises. Lady MacPhail doesn't have that much to look after.'

Emmett smiled, getting the man immediately.

'She said she's taking the carriages off to a friend.'

'Absolutely,' said Magnus. 'Disappointing to hear about the others being stolen, but we'll have some people travelling with ours. To be honest, we put little stake on it. They came with her, and she likes them in one of the dining rooms. I'll take you there now. You can see them. Do you know much about them yourself?'

'One of a collection of six, and they get increasingly large as you go from one to the other,' said Emmett. 'Although I work for the arts team, I'm not the specialist in the arts department. I'm a proper detective, in that sense.'

He thought Sabine and certainly Clarissa wouldn't like that comment. Although sometimes, Emmett felt he wasn't quite at home in the arts department, not knowing enough about it.

The place was full of staff, as maids seemed to run here and there, and he asked Magnus about it. 'She seems to have a full team here.'

'Lord MacPhail has a large staff throughout all his ventures. A number of them come back into the house in the winter. He has them working in shops and places he runs on various bits of his land, different shops for the tourists. So in the winter, some of them close and the staff come back into the house. They seem to like it. It works well. People get through their holidays. Generally, we don't have a lot of problems. He is a good employer, and I say that without prejudice,' said Magnus.

'That's nice to hear,' said Emmett, as he was led into a large wooden dining room. There he could see the two carriages. They were quite breathtaking: one about the size of a shoebox, the next almost double the size. Emmett could see how you could put one inside the other and stared at the jewels inside them.

'Do you know how much these are worth?' he asked.

'Her ladyship says they're priceless. I haven't been able to get a valuation, to be honest. His lordship's not that bothered about them.'

'Will you be coming with them tomorrow when they move?'

'No, it'll be some of the other staff that minds them. His lordship has an evening out that I need to be at.'

'I need to ask you something.'

'What do you need to ask me?'

'I need to ask you,' said Emmett, 'have you had any trouble recently around the place?'

'Not particularly. We have had some cases of a peeping tom.'

'A peeping tom?' said Emmett. 'What do you mean?'

'We've had a man watching the place, except they seem to watch, well, her ladyship.'

'Okay. Can you tell me a bit more about that?' said Emmett.

'Well, it started a month or two ago. Would appear at the outside walls, looking up. Been caught a few times staring with binoculars. He's usually in a quite a dirty mac, hood up. Sometimes there's a balaclava on. Chased him off. I think he's basically a pervert. His binoculars have been aimed at the rooms where Lady Angela's been getting changed. We caught him . . . well, we didn't catch him; we chased him once. He had got to her room, actually opened the door and then run.'

'Not easy to get in here though, is it?'

'No, and at the time, we had CCTV. It's gone now. We did report it down to your station, but I told them not to be that worried about it. We haven't seen him in a while though.'

'Can you describe him?'

'Not well. Very hairy, a lot of hair around the face when he didn't have the balaclava on. Quite a small frame, really, for a man.'

'Definitely a man's frame, though, was it?' asked Emmett.

'Couldn't say for sure, actually.'

'What makes you say it's a man, then?'

'Well, trying to look at her ladyship, wasn't he?'

'It is a modern day,' said Emmett.

'I suppose. But he did, well . . . he flashed her ladyship.'

'She didn't mention this when I was talking to her.'

'No, she won't. And I want you to keep it quiet. I'm only telling you because you've asked, so if you'd keep it quiet too. She can be quite sensitive about stuff like this.'

'And she said it was a man?'

'Well, not specifically. What she said to me was he flashed her, and she turned away. I did ask her to give a description of what she saw, which, you know, things like his chest. Was it hairy? Anything we could identify him by. It was rather an awkward conversation,' said Magnus. 'However, she gave next to no detail at all. I have a feeling she might have turned her back before he, well, exposed himself.'

'Okay,' said Emmett. The security chief gave him a description of what he had seen, pointing at places where the peeping Tom had been before Emmett made his way back to the car. As he sat down inside it, ideas were running through his head. There was something trying to connect. He just wasn't sure what it was.

Maybe Lady Angela could be at risk here, or rather her carriages, he thought. He dropped the handbrake of the car and headed back for Inverness. He would listen intently to what the others had found out when he got back.

Chapter 08

'S trange Seoras coming in last night, wasn't it?' Patterson gazed over at Clarissa, then gave a shake of his head and turned back to the road. 'I said, strange, that the boss was down.'

'How?' asked Patterson. 'He may wander in when he wants. He's the boss, isn't he? You wander over to my desk without asking. You wouldn't phone over.'

'No, he's up to something. He's wanting to keep an eye on me for some reason. He wants to—'

'What are you on about?' asked Patterson. 'It's just Macleod. He's down finding out what he wants to know. He'd obviously finished whatever he was going to do.'

'Were you there? He's putting his nose back in because he can't stay away from it, can he? Needs to be involved. He's watching what we're up to.'

'He said the chief constable was the one that requested this. Well, maybe he's—'

'What? Unsure if I can do it?'

'Well, you can be a bit—'

'A bit what, Pats?' asked Clarissa.

'It's not my place to say, is it?' said Patterson.

'No, you don't get to do that,' said Clarissa. 'You've opened your gob. Now what is it?'

'Well, you . . . I mean, you get the results. I'm not saying you don't; you do, but you also ruffle a few feathers on the way. Now, the chief constable's involved, and there's sort of high-up people. Maybe Macleod doesn't want you to be causing a bit of a fuss.'

'Causing a bit of a fuss? This is police work we're doing,' said Clarissa. 'We're not here trying to tidy up after the party, making sure that the people with the sore heads don't get disturbed. You know this is police work, Pats.'

'You asked,' said Patterson.

'I didn't know you looked at it like that,' said Clarissa.

'Now, you don't get to do that,' said Patterson suddenly. Clarissa looked back quickly, one eye on the road, one eye on Patterson.

'You don't get to do that to me,' he said. 'You asked me about what I thought. Don't take the hump because I told you what I thought, okay? You rush into places, you cause merry hell and it gets results. I've seen it. You even saved Macleod's life at one point because you didn't wait for other people. You went right in, and you got hold of it. He'll know that as much as I do. What's this insecurity you've got? What's this—'

'Do you know what it's like at the top, Pats?'

'Clearly not,' said Patterson.

'You become in charge of the team. You've got to manage the team. Got to keep the team happy. And then you've got this other person who comes in. You've got to keep them happy. Who's sorting you out? Who's looking after you?'

'Macleod looks after you.'

'Macleod works me. Puts me in a place where he knows I

can be of use,' said Clarissa.

'Puts you where your talents are best suited,' said Patterson.

'He's up to something,' said Clarissa suddenly.

'Chill out,' said Patterson. 'I mean it. Chill out. I'll always respect you,' said Patterson suddenly. 'I'll always have time for you. You saved my life, do things that others would run from. You're there where angels fear to tread. But see, sometimes you need to get over yourself and you need to just chill out and get on with it.'

Clarissa turned to snap back at him, but then she didn't. He was speaking his mind. She had asked for it. And to be fair, Pats had earned the right to speak with her. He was one of the team and he'd stood by her.

'Okay Pats, let's see what we can chill out over at Hamper Holdings.'

The little green sports car pulled up in front of the large industrial building. It was a massive warehouse and Clarissa and Patterson entered a small reception to be led upstairs to a boardroom. Once there, they were served coffee and made to wait for fifteen minutes until eventually a woman in a light blue blouse and black skirt entered.

She had blue glasses, large round ones, and white hair in a rough bob that hung down to the base of her neck. Although she was clearly older than Clarissa, she looked vibrant.

'Sorry to have kept you waiting, but it is a rather busy time,' said the woman. 'My name is Isabelle McNeice. I run Hamper Holdings. We're in the last days and it's full on. We've got last-minute deliveries to get out for Christmas. I've got a good team, but you need to be there. Things happen. I hope you understand. What is it I can help you with?'

'We're actually here to give you some information,' said

Clarissa. 'I believe you are the owner of the largest of the Cinderella carriages.'

'I am,' said Isabel, 'although I tend not to broadcast that too widely. All bought and paid for, mind. Got it in a secret auction, but there's paperwork to show ownership.'

'Well, I'm afraid I have to tell you,' said Clarissa, 'that the first two of the carriages, the two smallest ones, have been stolen from their respective owners. DC Patterson and myself, Detective Inspector Urquhart, are on the case to try to find them. However, due to the reticence of their owners to furnish us with information, we thought it best to warn all owners. One being taken looks like a simple theft, two looks like someone collecting.'

Isabel McNeice laughed.

'I'm afraid this is quite serious,' said Clarissa. 'I am an art lover myself and I realise the worth of these carriages.'

'Well, they're going to have a job nicking mine, aren't they?' said Isabel, laughing. 'It's a full-size carriage. I mean, how are they going to get it anywhere?'

'Where's it stored, if I may?' asked Patterson.

'Of course you may. It was constable, wasn't it?' Patterson nodded. 'It's actually on these premises, because at the moment we're getting it ready.'

'You keep it in the warehouse?' said Clarissa. 'It's a bit of a grandiose item for that.'

'It was getting prepared, to go into the Christmas parade in Inverness. It doesn't just need to look its best, it needs to be protected. Make sure we have the correct coverings here and there. We have to plan what to do if it rains. The largest carriage is a working carriage, unlike its more ornate sisters. You can store them all inside each other. Did you know that?'

said Isabel.

'Yes, yes, I did.'

'I'm sorry,' said Isabel. 'I really need to get back to work. Tell you what I'm going to do. I have a man who's looking after the carriage. He's called Davey. I'll get Davey to come up, take you down and show you.'

'Is he aware of the security arrangements for what's going on?' asked Patterson.

'There are not a lot of security arrangements. Nobody's going to nick this. Nobody will steal the carriage. It's too big, it's too obvious. We've got people with it all the time. I can understand how they could steal the smaller ones. I'm not worried about it,' said Isabel.

'Well, that's obviously your prerogative,' said Clarissa. 'I would disagree with your stance, though. So, please, I'm advising you to take good care of it and make sure somebody is with it over the next while.'

'You're going to have thousands of people looking at it,' said Isabel. 'Sorry, I must run. Stay here. Davey will be up in a minute.'

The woman turned and briskly raced out of the boardroom, leaving Clarissa and Patterson alone. Patterson raised his eyebrows while Clarissa shook her head.

'This is typical of the art world,' said Clarissa. 'People do not know what things are worth. But if it was me, I'd have a permanent guard.'

'No, you wouldn't,' said Patterson. 'Couldn't afford it.'

'Pats, if I could afford that carriage, I'd be able to afford the guard.'

'How do they afford the items, then?'

'Well, she's obviously got a thriving business,' said Clarissa.

'Anyway, we'll see what this Davey guy says.'

It took a few moments before a man opened the door and wandered in. He had brown shoes with blackish trousers that didn't really suit the shoes, complementing his jacket more. It was also brown but heavily creased. He wore a light, pale green shirt which allowed his stomach to protrude against the buttons. His hair was white and reminded Clarissa of a mad professor. It may have been brushed that morning, but obviously to no avail. However, he was reasonably jolly.

'Hello,' he said. 'You want to see her? I'll take you to see her. Not a problem.'

'You must be Davey,' said Clarissa.

'Davi. Davi,' said the man.

Unusual way of saying it, thought Clarissa.

'Okay, Davi. I'm Detective Inspector Clarissa Urquhart. This is Detective Constable Patterson. Please, lead on.'

A few times, Clarissa thought the man was going to fall over as he tootled along, but he always seemed to keep his balance. Various people got out of his way because Davi didn't stop for you. Instead, there was almost a reverence around him. Either that, or they were just clearing the way for mad old Granda.

He burst into a large room at the back of the building, and Clarissa raced through, followed by Patterson. The room itself was almost bare except for a couple of items sitting around. At the far end was a roller shutter door that was currently pulled down, but the room was dominated by the carriage. It was magnificent. The gold, the silver, the gleam. Clarissa was in awe. She stepped up close to it.

'Don't touch it,' said Davi suddenly. 'Don't touch it. It's getting ready for Christmas. Are you ready for Christmas yet? I'm ready for Christmas. The big day when he comes. But before that, the magic will happen.'

'The magic?' asked Patterson.

The man clapped his hands, and looked back to Patterson. 'She's going to go on parade, going to be pulled by horses. She's going to—'

'She's in the Inverness parade,' said Clarissa. 'We heard that. Miss McNeice said you were getting it ready.'

'So much to do. Clean, you see. Come, come,' said Davi, and he picked up a bottle of something and a cloth. 'Look here,' he said to Clarissa, pointing at something on the side of the carriage. 'That's not good. That has to be clear.'

He poured the solution onto the cloth and wiped, then he stepped back away from it.

'Ah, see, see how she comes up! See, of course we have to watch for the rain or the snow. I was worried, because it's so cold at night now, so cold in the parade. She'll be okay though. I've reinforced, treated the wood, because it's wood. It's wood underneath the paint, but all the jewels too and all the gold, some of it's leaf, some of it's wood.'

Clarissa was bombarded with detail about the carriage, but she was taking it all in. The man knew what he was talking about. He stepped back for a moment and turned to her.

'Coffee,' he said almost wildly. 'I get the coffee.' He shot out of the room, leaving Clarissa and Patterson with the carriage.

'What a nutter,' said Patterson. 'She seriously left this guy in charge?'

'Your ignorance about art is unbelievable,' said Clarissa. She turned to see a questioning Patterson. 'He may be eccentric, he may be off his trolley, but he knows what he's doing here. He's caring for this carriage in as good a way as I've seen lots of people do it. Everything he told me about it is true.'

She stepped back for a moment. Her heart was pounding, the blood running through her veins. This was the big one. This was the largest of the Cinderella carriages.

'Imagine being inside of this. Imagine being pulled along. This isn't art. Not just art. This is what art should be,' Clarissa said to Patterson. 'This is a dream. This is you lifted, your life gone on full, wild.'

The door opened and Davi walked back in. He was holding a tray with some plastic cups on it. He handed one to Patterson and then to Clarissa and then was going to take one himself when he suddenly put the tray on the floor.

'No milk,' he said to Patterson, and he shambled quickly off to the door, where he stopped and turned round. 'Do you take it?'

'Yes,' said Patterson.

Davi's fresh eyes shot over to Clarissa. 'Do you take it?'

'No,' said Clarissa.

'That's one then.' He disappeared out the door only to pop his head back in five seconds later. 'You, sugar?'

'Yes,' said Patterson.

'You, sugar?' he looked at Clarissa.

'No,' said Clarissa. Again, the man was off.

Clarissa sipped her coffee, aware that the plastic cups were pretty inadequate. The heat was coming through strongly, so much so that Patterson had actually put his down on the ground. When Davi came back and had sorted out the coffee, he stood beside Clarissa, admiring the carriage with her.

'How are you getting her there?'

'They're bringing her down in the lorry. I have to—well, it has to be done carefully. I have to get the right people.'

'I can understand that,' said Clarissa. 'You seem like the right man, though. You understand it. Have you spent a lot of time around the carriage?'

'Long time,' said the man. 'I understand it.'

He leaped forward, and gently put a hand on one of the wheels. Clarissa leaned forward as well, her hand touching the wheel. Davi looked at her and smiled. 'See? This is Christmas.'

The wood had slight imperfections, because the wheels had obviously been used. But as she looked inside the interior, the immaculate cloth, the jewel that sat on the seat. The carriage was incredibly strong, yet delicately cut. Perfect stanchions within the carriage.

'Magic,' Clarissa agreed. 'You're right, Davi. This is Christmas.'

'It's coming,' he said. 'It's coming.' Once again, he clapped his hands.

Chapter 09

'Are we all back?' asked Clarissa, sweeping into the office. A quick glance around told her that Emmett and Sabine had already arrived. She looked at her desk and there was a cup of coffee and a slice of Christmas cake.

'Who put that out?' asked Clarissa.

'That's from Emmett,' said Sabine. 'I think the correct term is "thank you."'

Clarissa reached down and broke the Christmas cake in half. She then picked up a piece, ate some, and chewed on it thoughtfully before putting it back down.

'Emmett, where did you get this? It's fantastic.'

'I thought you needed it. You seemed a little hassled, especially last night.'

'I'm fine, but thank you,' said Clarissa. She dropped her handbag on the side of the chair and sat down on it.

'So, what have we got?' she asked.

'Well, Katie Grouse,' said Ferguson, 'bought hers from an Oliver Davitt in a secret auction.'

'Mine was bought in a secret auction as well,' said Emmett.

'That's funny. So was ours,' said Clarissa.

'It is, isn't it?' said Patterson. 'I think they all bought them off the same person.'

'Hang on a minute,' said Emmett. 'Do you think at some point these carriages were actually all together? Do you think somebody actually owned all of them?'

'The history is not clear,' said Clarissa. 'Especially the more recent history. At one point, they were all together, then they were split up again, then they were back together. And we go into a more shady part of their history. There's a time when their whereabouts is unknown, and that's when they become more of a myth—although never truly, because they existed, obviously. Then they've reappeared. Or at least, that was the rumour. And we've confirmed that. It wasn't difficult to find out, certainly these last four. I think the first two would have been harder to find, although there were rumours they had them.'

'So, are we any further forward?' asked Emmett.

'Not particularly,' said Clarissa. 'What did you guys get?'

'Well, if I can finish,' said Sabine. 'Katie Grouse has it displayed very much in the open. She has a secure room with pictures and items. But she doesn't seem to care about the carriage. It's almost as if it's just an awkward object and she puts it somewhere nice. It looked genuine to me. I did check the carriage.'

'What about you, Emmett? Did yours look genuine?' said Clarissa.

'I wouldn't have a clue,' said Emmett. 'Lady Angela lives in a rather strange building. Modern and yet trying to be old. She feels very fake to me. Acts like a lady, but really there's not a lot of substance to it. However, she has a lot of security around her. Many people are in the building. The carriages are in a dining room in her house. There's plenty of people going past. Plenty of people about. She, of course, has the two carriages. They are, however, going to a friend's tomorrow night. To be honest, I don't know if it's wise. They are going to be on display.

'The security man who works there, Magnus, won't be with them, but he says there'll be people taking them there. I've got to be honest. I wouldn't like to try to steal them from her home.'

'You warned her about the imminent threat?' asked Clarissa.

'Of course I did. She's also had a peeping Tom. I think that's something that interests me.'

'Interests you?' blurted Clarissa.

'Not the best way to put it,' said Emmett. 'The peeping Tom apparently flashed Lady Angela, but he's been watching the house over the last few months. Hasn't been back recently. Just interests me—I don't know,' said Emmett. 'We'll see if the connection comes.'

'Well, Pats and I saw the biggest carriage. It's being cared for by an old man, but someone who knows his art. Called Davi.'

'Is that like 'Davy'?' said Sabine. 'We have Davy down in Glasgow.'

'No, I called him Davey. He said, "Davi." He was very insistent about it. Anyway, Davi knows what he's doing. It's kept in the warehouse. There's lots of people about, even if it's in its own room. It's also going to be moved by a lorry and taken down to the parade. I think I'm going to go to the parade organisers and talk to them, just to see what the arrangements are on that side. That would seem to be a good chance to steal it if it's down towards the parade. Although, as Isabel McNeice said, there were lots and lots of people there. It's going to have lots of eyes on it.'

'So, how many people were in the room looking after it?' asked Emmett.

'Just Davi. Although, if you opened up the shutter doors, I think it goes out into the freight yard. So, everybody would see.'

'Everybody would see,' said Patterson. 'Listen, they're also working a twenty-four-hour shift at the moment. All the way right up to Christmas. They're getting these hampers done. Very clever hampers, too. It's a big business. Isabel McNeice, the owner, seemed to be flat out working. Davi, however . . . Clarissa says he was good with the carriage, but to be quite honest, he was like a child. Banging on about Christmas, all about the wonder of the carriage.'

'That's why you're a philistine, Pats,' Clarissa said. 'It was wonderful. I got to touch the wheel. I got to stand with it. It was amazing.'

Clarissa looked over at a smiling Sabine. She knew it was what the two of them shared. For as much as Sabine looked so different—young, physically fit, and probably more the type of person the hierarchy would want running the department— Clarissa and Sabine understood their art, marvelled in the joy of it.

Pats wasn't there yet, maybe he never would be, and as for Emmett, she didn't know. The man painted little models; yes, the man played imaginary games. She didn't have qualms with him about his detective work, but Clarissa didn't understand his life outside of work.

'It's going to be hard to steal these big ones, isn't it?' said Patterson. 'I mean, even the smaller ones. It's getting harder and harder. You don't just nick it and put it in your pocket.

You're going to have to be carrying it out of places. They're going on show to a lot of places as well. I don't get how this is going to be achieved.'

'Well, we've warned them,' said Clarissa. 'We have done that, at least. There'll be more eyes on them. People will be more aware and won't take any risks.'

'Is that cake?' said a voice from the door. Clarissa looked up and saw Macleod.

'Would you like a piece?' asked Emmett. Macleod nodded and walked into the room.

'We're in the middle of a briefing,' said Clarissa suddenly.

'Oh, apologies,' said Macleod, 'but that's excellent. I could do with one. The Chief Constable has been on again. Wants an update.'

'Well, we're all just back from seeing the owners of the rest of the carriages. We're just discussing what to do.'

Patterson quickly brought Macleod up to speed, when asked to by Clarissa.

'Good,' said Macleod. 'Everybody's warned, everybody knows, but are we any further to finding out who did it?'

'Not at the moment, Seoras,' said Clarissa. 'We aren't exactly being helped by these owners.'

'Appreciate that,' said Macleod, 'but the Chief Constable's jumping on this one, and if we can get him on board, we might get him to help us.'

Macleod said this out loud, almost absentmindedly, and Clarissa looked over at him. 'You've gone on about this several times now. How is he going to help us?'

'Plans,' said Macleod. 'Plans. Oh, by the way, Emmett, this is a rather good Christmas cake.'

'Well, I bought it in a shop,' said Emmett.

'Proper shop, though,' said Sabine.

'So what's your next move?' said Macleod. 'I mean, you visited the owners. You said they're not being any help to you. This is the arts world. Where are the first two? Where have they gone? I take it you know how to get stuck into that.'

'Of course I know how to get stuck into that,' said Clarissa. 'Emmett and Sabine are going to hit some dealers. Find out if anything's being moved.' She looked over at Sabine. 'Properly. No phone calls. Get into the underground. See if anything's being moved through there. It'll be done on the quiet. So, you'll have to—'

'I know,' said Sabine. 'I'll have to go in and rattle a few cages. Emmett's good at that.'

Clarissa looked over at Emmett. He had taken off the raincoat, and Clarissa could see his white shirt and black trousers. He looked like somebody who was getting ready for a funeral. Either that, or someone ready for the school concert. He just hadn't applied the tie.

She looked at Sabine. The woman had her jeans on. She could throw that hip look. Sabine had style. Yes, it was that younger style, the one the top brass liked. It wasn't Clarissa's style, but then Clarissa was a free-thinking woman. She always felt Sabine was still trying to follow the trend, not set it. She wasn't annoyed at this—more, pitied the woman for it.

'What are *you* going to do?' said Macleod.

'Getting to that,' said Clarissa touchily. 'I'm going to see the organisers of the Inverness Parade. Pats and I will work that way, and we're going to watch where these other carriages are going. Two of them are going to a soiree at somebody's house. The large carriage is going to the Inverness Christmas Parade, so we stay on top. We need to shake a few people down.'

'What about this secret auction?' asked Macleod. 'Have we found out any more about that?'

'That's going to be tough,' said Clarissa. 'It's a secret auction for a reason. They won't say who's been there; obviously, they were themselves. They say who it's sold by—it was Oliver Davitt. Maybe we can try to find him.'

'I guess that'll be me,' said Patterson.

'Absolutely,' said Clarissa. 'You're on the computers. Get more records of the owners of the carriages now we've met them; get a bit into their history. We know where they are now. Let's find out exactly where they came from.'

'Well, it's all looking good,' said Macleod. 'If I can have a word—'

'Of course,' said Clarissa. 'If the rest of you give us the room—'

'No,' said Macleod. 'Come up to my office after you've seen these guys before they head off to Glasgow, or wherever you're sending them.'

He stood up and walked out, and Clarissa looked around at the others before she stood up and followed him.

Macleod's office looked immaculate as Clarissa walked in. The man was sitting behind his large desk and put a phone call through for coffee. Two cups arrived from his secretary, whom he thanked, and once the door was shut, he turned to look at Clarissa.

'Emmett, what do you think of him?'

'What?' asked Clarissa.

'Emmett, what do you think of Emmett?'

'I don't get him. I don't get his outside life. The man paints miniature figures. He's aloof at times, not like a normal copper. You know, I mean, take you, for instance,' said Clarissa.

'You're deadly serious. Yes, you can be fun, but you've got that determination. Got that, well, no-nonsense attitude.'

'And Emmett doesn't?'

'He's quite weird, I guess. I mean, look at the way he's dressed today.'

'He doesn't know how to dress. You're telling me the most you've come up with working with him is he doesn't know how to dress?'

'Sabine likes him. Sabine really likes him,' said Clarissa. 'I've seen that. She enjoys working with him. But he's . . . well, he comes at things differently, doesn't he? Very much takes in the whole. He seems to explore ideas when he's solving stuff that I wouldn't go down. Certainly doesn't like to kick up a fuss.'

'Do you want him on your team long term?'

'Are you cutting people from my team already?' she said.

'Chief Constable wants this case done. If I can get it done, or rather if you can get it done, you'll be opening up some possibilities. We've got things within the departments that need tidied up. I need excellent officers to do that. And I already made a start. I put you in the arts department.'

Clarissa looked at him. 'And you want to take two staff off me?'

'You were under Hope for a long time,' said Macleod. 'I developed Hope up, and she's now the DI. I helped develop you up, I think. I want to develop you more. You're the DI in the arts department. I need somebody for something else.'

'You think Emmett might be that person?'

'Possibly,' said Macleod, 'but what I do need is to get the Chief Constable on board and, well, he needs to see us being successful. He needs to see these other types of people. He's very firm-minded about what he wants. I don't like that. I have a team and I've always had a team that expands and brings in people who are very different. That's how we solve cases.'

'Well, if you take him, I want somebody in return.'

'That's fine and you can get them, but it's not happening yet. I wanted you to understand why I'm jumping on you at the moment. Go solve this for me. I know it's tough. I know you're not getting the right help from the people involved, but solve it. Bring me what I need, and I'll get you who you want.'

Clarissa stood up, turned to walk to the door, but Macleod shouted after her. 'Oh, by the way, Frank's fine.'

She stopped and looked at him. 'What's that meant to mean?'

'You gave me a hassle for barging in on your mince pie. And then you bolted out the door when I mentioned the carriages.'

'Well, he understands. He knows what the art means to me. He knows.'

'Yes, he does. And that's good,' said Macleod. 'Don't forget him. Whenever I'm in the middle of my cases, I get a nudge from the office outside, from that desk and that wonderful lady who keeps me right. Make sure somebody keeps you right. We all need it.'

Clarissa stood looking at him. 'Thanks, Seoras,' she said, and closed the door behind her.

Chapter 10

Clarissa had sent Emmett and Sabine back down to Glasgow because there was no way for them to tap into the underground simply by phoning around. They would need to talk to the correct people, and the correct people might not want to talk to them. She felt bad about racing them back and forward across the country, but they were young, unlike her. And maybe that's what they were for. Macleod did that. He sat back and put his pawns out. She'd have to stop talking in these chess metaphors. It really wasn't good. They were people, after all.

Patterson was deep into his computer work. Clarissa simply left him, not wishing to disturb him. Instead, feeling guilty, she made a phone call to Frank, who she found was at the golf club. He wasn't working, simply there having a cup of coffee with the lads. He said he was fine and was organising the food for their Christmas day. Part of her missed that. She was going to do so much with Frank. This was going to be their time off. But in truth, she was buzzing.

She'd got to see a Cinderella carriage, the big one. Got to touch it, got to be up close. That was only dampened by the idea it was now going to go out on full show. With that in mind, she contacted the organiser of the Christmas parade, one Deborah McGovern. She was operating out of a small office in the centre of Inverness. Clarissa parked the little green sports car in one of the multi-storey car parks before walking along to the woman's office.

The streets were snow covered, but it wasn't deep, having been worked down by many people. Shopping was in full flow despite the difficulties of getting around in the snow. That was the thing about the north of Scotland—it had snow frequently; it knew how to deal with it. Large parts of the UK went to pot because of a drop of snow; here, well, they knew what to do, and they got on with it.

Clarissa liked the snow. It made everything more picturesque. Even the old city she marched along looked better with the snow around. Of course, when the temperatures rose, and it went slushy and the ice came, that wouldn't be good. Now, because the temperatures were cold and the snow wasn't falling, it instead left what she described as perfect winter conditions.

Clarissa found the office of the parade, which at one point had obviously been a shop. The interior had been gutted and now was being taken over temporarily by the parade organisers. As she walked through the front door, several young people ran about, holding bits of paper, passing them here and there. She tried to stop one of them, but most of them seemed to be too busy. She noticed a young man at a desk in the corner.

'You,' said Clarissa. 'I'm DI Urquhart. I'm here to see Mrs McGovern.'

'Who?' said the man.

'Mrs McGovern. Deborah McGovern.'

'Debbie?' said the man. 'You want to see Debbie?'

'Yes, I would like to see Debbie,' said Clarissa.

'Debbie's through the back.' He turned away and started looking at his phone. Clarissa felt a rage build up inside her. She marched over to the desk.

'What's your name?'

'I'm sorry,' said the man, still looking at his phone.

'I said, what's your name? Me, I'm DI—that's Detective Inspector—Clarissa Urquhart, here to see Mrs McGovern.'

'Yeah, I told you, Debbie's in the back.'

'What's your name?' asked Clarissa.

'Mark,' he said.

'I suggest, Mark, you get up off your backside and you take me through to see Mrs McGovern. Are you getting paid for this?'

'Yeah, more than minimum wage as well.'

'Then get off your arse and show me through.'

The man looked at her. He could have only been about eighteen or nineteen. Clarissa was leaning over the desk now.

'Off your arse,' said Clarissa, in the most quietly threatening voice she'd ever produced. 'Take me through.'

Slowly, the man got up, his phone put away into his pocket. Clarissa followed him through to the rear of the building and to an office door. He went to open it.

'Is she in there?' asked Clarissa.

'She is,' the man said.

Clarissa stepped forward, and took his hand off the door-knob. 'This is how you do it,' she said.

She rapped on the windowpane of the door and heard a 'Come in.'

'Now you open it, you take me through, and you tell her who

I am.' The man was looking at her, almost in disbelief, but with a slight amount of fear behind it. *That's good*, thought Clarissa. She followed him in and stood there as he announced her.

'Debbie, this is DC Carrie Hart.'

Clarissa glowered at the man. 'It's Detective Inspector Clarissa Urquhart. And I think Mark needs more training.'

'That's fine, Mark—off you go.'

The woman behind the desk stepped out from behind it. She wore a jumper and jeans and had long, brown, flowing hair, but she had a big smile too. Mark left, closing the door behind him as Clarissa shook hands.

'Debbie McGovern. Sorry about that, Detective Inspector. We have to take some of them on. It's to do with the charities that are involved in the parade. I'm afraid Mark's not one of their better examples.'

'Can't be easy,' Clarissa said, 'having to work with . . . well . . .'

'Hopefully, he gets something from it,' said Debbie. 'How can I help you?'

She went to speak. The phone rang and Debbie apologised, putting her hand up before grabbing the phone. Two minutes later, after a rather heated conversation, she turned back to Clarissa.

'Sorry, how can I—' The door opened. A young woman stood there.

'Debs, the posters aren't coming through right. They're not properly done.'

'I'll be with you in a minute,' said the woman. 'I need to talk to the Detective Inspector.'

'So, what do I do?' said the woman.

'Just hold on.'

'But Debs, I need you now.'

Clarissa stepped beyond Debbie, in front of the young woman. She was slightly smaller than Clarissa, but Clarissa's shoulders were up, the shawl presenting Clarissa as some formidable object. Her eyes were raging.

'Your boss just told you she needs to speak to me. She will be speaking to me in peace. You will go back, and you will talk to whoever has produced these posters and you will tell them they are not correct. You will ask them to give you the correct thing and to produce it properly. Okay?'

The woman looked up at Clarissa. 'I can't do that.'

'You can. Detective Inspector Clarissa Urquhart is telling you, you can. And you will. And then, after I have left, you will give Debbie an update on that. Okay? That's what you do. That is work.'

'But I need—'

'You don't,' said Clarissa. The woman sheepishly left the office, and Clarissa turned back. 'Sorry,' she said. 'I couldn't help it.'

'No,' said Deborah, almost laughing. 'It's manic here, abso-lutely manic. I'm working with people who need to be brought on a lot. They're not very—well, not incompetent, but they need a lot of handholding.'

'If I didn't have the case, I'd come in and give you a hand,' said Clarissa. 'Crack a whip. Not enough whips crack these days. Back in my day, you knew what you had to do, and you had to darn well do it.'

'I suppose you got a kick up the backside if you didn't,' said Deborah.

'Or a thick ear,' said Clarissa.

'Can't do that these days,' said Deborah. 'You'll have to teach me that stare, though.'

'Can you tell me about the Cinderella carriage that's being used in your parade?'

'The Cinderella carriage? Oh, don't—it's a delightful idea but I mean, it's expensive, difficult to insure. How do you insure it?'

'You don't want it there?' said Clarissa.

'Of course we want it there! It's a highlight. I mean, I don't know much about it, but apparently it's an absolute gem of a piece.'

'I know lots about it,' said Clarissa. 'It is—for an art lover, it's incredible.'

'But it also looks superb for the public. I mean, this is Christmas. It's a Christmas parade. We're trying to bring glitz, glamour. It's meant to be about fairy tales, it's meant to be about best wishes coming true. Can you imagine the little kids seeing this carriage, especially the girls?'

Clarissa hadn't really thought about it like that, and yet, maybe she had. Maybe she was that little girl when she had touched it.

'Are you able to cover the insurance and things?'

'Hamper Holdings is covering all that side. I told them we couldn't, but they seem to be quite happy. There's been a lot of people pushing for it to be in the parade. I'm not sure the idea originally came from Hamper Holdings, but they seem to have gone with it.'

'How are you looking after it?'

'Well, you've got to get it down, haven't you? So Hamper Holdings, we've let deal with that side of it. There's a guy up there—Davi?'

'Yes, I've met Davi,' said Clarissa.

'Well, Davi's organised getting it here. Once it's here, we have premises acquired—old fire station, actually. It's going to be held in there for the best part of a day. Davi will be with it. That's where the horses will come to pick it up from. He knows how to attach the horses. He knows how to ride the carriage and he'll dress up. In fact, he's—well, who else could you put on the front of it except Santa?

'You know, most of the phone calls I get at the moment are about the carriage. We're trying to keep it publicised and yet secret about where we're going with it and what we're doing. Because, you can imagine, many people want to see it. Some people won't want to just see it at the parade; they want to see it before, they want to get close, they want to touch it. But an item like that, you have to keep some sort of distance.'

'Absolutely,' said Clarissa, almost feeling guilty for having touched it herself.

'I've had to get some of my better people to deal with that side. That's why I've got a lot of these newbies and people from the charities that have been given to me, dealing with other things that are not so important. You screw a poster up, it doesn't cost you much. We mess this up, we could damage what is, I've been told, a priceless item.'

'It is, but more in a sense, without price—we don't know how to price it,' said Clarissa.

'Well, that's why I said the insurance and plans had to come from Hamper Holdings. It's their owner who is—well, she's the one who is covering it all off. She's put so much money into this parade. If you see our poster, it's about time. Hamper Holdings are up there; they're bang, you know, right on it. She's going to come along and do a bit on the stage that night when we get the parade done. We need to be good, we need to make a big parade after last time. What went wrong on stage, with that—well, that killer of a Santa Claus. I can't believe they stopped that. That could have been horrific.

'In fact—' Deborah stood and looked at the moment at Clarissa. 'You were involved, weren't you? I recognise you now. You were—'

'I used to work for the . . . what we describe as the murder team. But I've moved. I'm working with the arts team now. I'm the head of it.'

'Oh, right! That's why you're looking at the carriage? But . . . but why? I mean . . . What's wrong at the moment?'

'The Cinderella carriage you are working with,' said Clarissa, 'is one of six. You're going to be getting the biggest one. It goes right down to the smallest one you can hold in the palm of your hand. They're all capable of fitting inside each other. Unfortunately, the first two have recently been stolen.'

'Really?' said Deborah. 'Are you worried that—'

'Yes, frankly,' said Clarissa. 'We have concerns. The carriage you're getting is very difficult to steal, though. It's so big, and that's why I'm chasing through what's going to happen with it. By the sounds of it, Hamper Holdings are dealing with it all, because you're going to have Davi with it the whole way through. It'll be very hard to steal it. Except forcibly. And that will not be easy. I mean, it's such a big carriage. To get away with it, to put it somewhere, is so difficult. You'll have so many eyes on it once it comes down from Hamper Holdings.'

'Exactly,' said Deborah. 'But I'm glad now they're looking after it. I don't need that headache. I've got enough going on. Do you know what it's like trying to sort out fireworks behind a stage?'

'I honestly don't,' said Clarissa. 'But give me a copy of your plans for what's happening with it once it arrives down with Davi to that old fire station.'

'I will do,' said Deborah.

Clarissa handed over a card, telling her to email the said plans before Clarissa shook her hand. As she opened the door to leave Deborah's office, Clarissa saw at least five people milling about. They raced into the office once Clarissa had left it. She couldn't help herself. She turned back and stuck her head in the door.

'Excuse me. Your boss would like one at a time, please. All of you, back out here.'

There was a moment where they looked and stared at her, but Clarissa kept a sullen face. One by one, they walked back out.

'In a line,' she said. Once they'd lined up, she told the first to go through. 'And the rest of you, don't move until that door opens again. And then one by one, you go in and you take what you need in with you and you talk to your boss. That room is your boss's kingdom. You do not enter until asked,' she said.

She shook her head at them and then marched off, out of the door. She could hear the swearing behind her. And a smile crossed her lips.

Chapter 11

Sabine stood outside the pub, looking at Emmett. They'd returned to Glasgow and briefly changed. As she was about to enter a pub, she'd dressed in her jeans, long boots, and leather jacket. Her long hair had been brushed and was now hanging behind her. Emmett was standing beside her, dressed in his blue jeans and T-shirt, a couple of large dice motifs on the front. *Nothing about Emmett ever looked cool,* Sabine thought. He was just Emmett. Even the trainers he was wearing were so he could run, as he put it to her. He didn't like running in shoes. It didn't feel good.

Sabine stood idly chatting with Emmett, not saying much, because, in truth, they were watching the pub entrance. The pub was in the city centre, but it was in a back alley, and wasn't a pub that Sabine would have frequented. Instead, it was what they would have called a spit and sawdust pub, one where fights broke out regularly. One in which men sat and drank themselves to oblivion. There wasn't really a large social scene around it. It was just a den where you could drink your sorrows dry, as long as you didn't mind possibly getting a punch in the face at some point.

Sabine had heard about some of these pubs. Somebody

didn't like the look of you, and suddenly you got a fist to the face, or worse still, a glass. Uniform talked about them a lot, and in her earlier days, she'd attended the scenes of post-drinking fights. However, this was the pub that Haulage frequented.

'That's him,' said Ferguson. Emmett stepped forward, before twisting around and throwing his arms around Sabine in what looked like a romantic hug. Instead, he was scanning over her shoulder, watching the man entering the pub.

'Shall we both go in?' he said to her.

'No, I'll go in from the front,' said Sabine. 'He's liable to run out the back. You go round to the rear. It comes out onto the adjoining alley on the other side. I'll give you two minutes.'

'Okay,' said Emmett, and his hand slipped off her. There was nothing in what he did except good acting. She knew plenty of other officers who liked her and who would have probably held that hug a little longer, if not tried something else. She felt totally safe with Emmett, which said something, not that she couldn't handle herself with the others. To actually feel that about someone—was there anyone else she felt like that with? Yes, there was—Macleod, for instance. But he was an old man, compared to Emmett.

She stood waiting outside and watched as a group of guys walked past her, one asking what she was doing this evening. She gave them the stare. If they had reacted negatively to that, she would have said some things before revealing who she was. But she didn't want to, and so she ignored the next quip that came back as the men walked on.

Sabine raised her hands up and brushed back her hair again before stepping forward into the pub. As she opened the door, she heard the swearing on the left-hand side. Two men were having an argument. It hadn't come to blows yet. On the right-hand side, somebody was off their stool, lying on the floor. She wasn't sure if he was going to get back up. One man was looking at her, eyes roaming up and down her body, but she didn't have time to stop and teach him a lesson.

Instead, her eyes roamed to the back of the pub, and there she saw him—Haulage. He was dressed smartly, although in the sense that your grandfather would dress smartly after he'd had a few. The suit looked neat enough, but the handkerchief coming out of the breast pocket was completely in the wrong place, unfolded and looked a mess. The hat the man was wearing was the wrong colour, and his shoes—his shoes were cheap. And now he was looking right back at Sabine.

Sabine didn't take her gaze off him. A man stood up from a chair beside Sabine and said, 'Where are you off to, gorgeous?'

She didn't have time, so her left hand came out. She went straight for his chest and pushed him back into the seat. 'Another time,' she said absently. Some men stopped now and looked, but they didn't react to her. Clearly, Sabine was on a mission for something, and they weren't wanting to get in the way.

Haulage watched her approach, and then jumped out of his seat and ran for the rear door. Sabine didn't run after him. Instead, she walked coolly on through until she reached the rear door of the pub. It was an emergency exit, but everyone used it anyway. As she stepped outside into the alleyway, she looked to the right towards the main street, but could see no one. When she looked left, there was Emmett, still sporting his Dice Motif t-shirt underneath the jacket. But up against the wall was Haulage. There were handcuffs on him, and Emmett with one hand was pushing him hard against the wall.

'Excellent,' said Sabine when she arrived. 'You don't know my new associate, do you?' Sabine smiled into the face of Haulage. He gave a quick shake of his head.

'That's not fair. That's not fair. Is she here?'

'Do you want her to be here?' asked Sabine.

Clarissa had an aura amongst many of the dealers—those who knew what she truly was, those who understood that when let loose, she would go for them. Yes, they all ran from Sabine. They fled from Clarissa.

'Got some questions for you, Haulage,' said Ferguson.

'You're not getting any answers,' said Haulage. 'Don't speak to filth like you.'

Emmett pushed harder with his hand. Haulage's face squashed up against the wall.

'We don't speak to the ladies like that, please,' said Emmett. He didn't look like much, silent, unassuming, but Emmett could make his presence felt.

'There's been a few thefts recently,' said Sabine.

'Well, it's not me. I took nothing.'

'You never do,' said Sabine. 'You move it on—hence Haulage, hence the man that shifts it to the next person. Thing is, the things that have been taken, big pieces. Big pieces, Haulage.' said Sabine. 'Cinderella's carriages.' There was a silence before Haulage half-twisted his head.

'Cinderella's carriages. Somebody's got them?'

Sabine looked into the man's eyes. Was he bluffing, or were his eyes alive at the thought of maybe getting a piece of the action? Was he hoping that he'd walk away from this and then find out where the carriages were? Or was he just bluffing?

'What do you know about them?' said Emmett, his hand still pushing the man up against the wall.

'Nothing. I have no knowledge of them. I didn't know they were taken until you said so.'

'And yet, you ran,' said Sabine. 'Why did you run?'

'Because you were there. If you're coming for me, there must be something up.'

'Oh no,' said Sabine. 'You have stopped and talked to me before. You've even stopped and talked to her before. Haulage, you flinched. You don't normally run from me. Not that quick, anyway. What's going on?'

'Nothing,' said Haulage.

Emmett's hand pushed harder.

'All right, quit it,' said Haulage. Emmett relaxed his hand, only slightly.

'All right, quit it. I heard they were gone. Of course, I heard they were taken. Everybody knows they were stolen. You don't get ripples like that. Find out, don't you? You find out.'

'And what did you find out?' said Sabine. 'You get a piece of the action?'

'Don't want a piece of the action. Mr Garrick is involved. Mr Garrick's not a delightful piece of work. A man with a lot of money. If he thought I'd taken his item, he would . . .'

'What?' said Emmett. 'Send the heavies round?'

'Heavies? Heavies, I can handle. Dealt with heavies all my life. No, no. Mr Garrick's not a man to send the heavies in. He'd send the executioner. One person. You won't see it coming, won't have a chance to bribe them, offer them money, get out of it. You'll be dead. Like that. That's Mr Garrick's style. He's so secretive, so quiet, hidden away. That's why I ran. I thought you might come from Garrick.'

'No, you didn't,' said Sabine.

'No. But Garrick has people everywhere. And if you're

investigating me, you might think I've had something to do with it.'

'And that's enough to run, is it?' said Emmett.

'Tell your friend, tell Dice Man here, that Mr Garrick has friends on both sides of the fence, legal and underground. Mr Garrick doesn't take prisoners. I don't move Garrick's stuff. Not unless Garrick asks. And if he asks, he's not asking.'

'So you're telling me you haven't been involved?'

'Not at all,' said Haulage. 'I wondered why, though. You know? So, I checked. There's been no soundings about it. Look, Ferguson. This is strange. There's been nothing. No soundings. No requests. I checked my rivals. I checked everything to see if anybody else was involved. You know?'

'So you could drop them in it,' said Emmett.

'Damn right. If Mr Garrick can get his stuff back, he'll pay well for it.'

'What have you got against Garrick?' asked Sabine.

'You and her. You think you know this world so well. Don't mess with Garrick. All right? Lots of friends, lots of influence. You just don't mess with Garrick. Because you don't see them coming.'

Ferguson gave a nod to Emmett, and he took his hand off Haulage.

'Keep out of it,' said Sabine. 'Whenever it comes down, just keep out of it. I wouldn't like to see a nice man like you end up in trouble.'

'Don't you worry,' said Haulage. 'I don't pick the bad ones. This would be a bad one.'

The pair watched Haulage walk away and then returned to the main street. They stopped off in a late-night cafe. As they sat together, Emmett asked Sabine about what had just happened.

'Is that normal? Did you expect that reaction from him?'

'No,' she said. 'I told you to wait outside, and to be honest, I thought he would talk to me. One of the reasons I didn't want you in with me was because he didn't know you. He knows what I am. He knows what I do. And he wouldn't be behind the door feeding me some information about others if they were up to anything. The fact he's saying that nobody knows anything—I actually believe him. He's not normally like that. I mean, Clarissa scares the life out of him. But he's not like that.'

'So what does it mean, then?' asked Emmett. 'I mean, can you just hold on to these carriages?'

'You could do,' said Sabine, 'but you've got to put it somewhere. Who's been involved? Who's been involved in shifting it? You would get a team normally. Names come out. Even rumours, at least. There are no rumours. There's nothing. I'll check the rest of the contacts, but Haulage is usually right about stuff. And if he's being that open, and he's saying he's not touching it, I'm not sure anybody else is.

'Haulage knows everything. He can move items wherever you want, when you want. But he also knows who else is moving stuff. It's his business. Maybe he doesn't like who's doing it. Quite often he drops them in it? Not a friendly man.'

'No, he's not,' Emmett said. Sabine sat back while Emmett sat forward in his chair.

'If there's nothing happening, if there's no particular action, nobody seems to move the items about,' said Emmett; 'then, if someone's going to hold on to them, why would they do that? They'd have to be a collector, wouldn't they?'

'Absolutely. They could be a collector, but you'd still have to shift it. I mean, at the moment you've got two small items.

You could take them yourself and you could put them away yourself, but to actually move some of the other ones, well, they're getting bigger. You might need help. And the rumours would be there. There would be a trail of some sort, even if it was just vague, even if it was just "I saw somebody talking to someone." Colleagues would be right onto that.'

'Maybe it's one of the owners. Maybe somebody's trying to bring the set together who already has one.'

'That's a thought,' said Sabine, 'but there's no evidence against the others.'

'No, there isn't.'

They finished their coffee and set out into the Glasgow night. It was cold, perishing, and Sabine was dressed like all the lunatics did when they went out to the pub in the cold Glasgow weather. Sabine shivered causing a glance from Emmett.

'I'm good,' she said.

'Are you sure you don't want my coat?'

'How are you not frozen?' asked Sabine.

'Keep on the move,' said Emmett.

Sabine looked at him. He had a pair of gloves on at the moment. They looked fat, far too fat for his hands, especially at the palms.

'You're not cold at all?'

'Not really,' said Emmett.

He lifted his gloved hands and put them up to her cheeks. She could feel the heat resonating through the glove.

'Heat warmers,' he said. 'Great stuff. You should try some.'

Sabine laughed. *Why hadn't she thought of that?*

Chapter 12

'I'm home, Frank!'

Clarissa slammed the door behind her. Her feet were tired. Her shoulders ached, and the case wasn't getting on as quickly as it should. But she had nothing to do. And so, she thought she should pop home, at least for an hour or two, and see Frank. Then she would go to bed and get back to the case in the morning.

'You want anything?' shouted Frank.

'Cup of tea would be lovely,' said Clarissa. She took off her shawl, hanging it up underneath the stairs. By the time she made it to the living room, she saw there was a cup of tea already waiting for her.

'How did you know?'

'Heard the car. Kettle was already boiled,' said Frank. 'Seat's ready for you.' It was a long sofa, and the corner of it was where Clarissa liked to be. Except she liked to be there in front of Frank.

'You take the seat first,' she said. Frank sat down, pushing himself into the corner of the sofa.

Clarissa sat down almost on top of him. She felt his arms go around her. She reached over to pick up her cup of tea and sip it. His chin was digging into her shoulder as she put the cup of tea to her mouth. She put the tea down before taking his hands in hers.

'Just had my ear bent by the chief constable. "How are we getting on? Where are we at?" Also had a call from Sabine telling me that the guy who's got the chief constable onto this isn't exactly pristine either. Akin to ordering hitmen at times.'

'But the job's going okay?' said Frank with worry.

'It's going fine, Frank. It's going fine. Don't worry about me. Oh, and you'll never guess what. Cinderella's carriage—got to touch it. The big one. I got to touch it. I was standing with it, Frank. It's amazing. It's—'

She felt the squeeze around her as he pulled her in tight. Then a kiss arrived on her neck.

'Maybe we'll talk about that later,' said Frank.

Clarissa leaned back. She turned her head and kissed him, and then sat, wrapped up in his lap. For about five minutes they didn't speak, as he burrowed his head into the side of her neck. They were older. Back in the day, she'd run up the stairs into bed. Not these days. These days she wanted a cuddle and a cup of tea. Eventually, she let out a sigh.

'Do my shoulders, Frank, would you?' she asked.

Almost instantly, his hands appeared on her shoulders and rubbed them. Frank was good. The man had terrific hands, and what he could do with her shoulders beat what any of the boys used to do for her back in the day. She laughed at herself—she must be getting old when a shoulder rub was all she wanted.

Clarissa could hear her phone vibrating. She looked around to see where she'd put it; then she realised it was still in her pocket. However, when she reached down, it wasn't there. Her hands went down close to it and found the phone vibrating on the sofa. She picked it up.

It was a call from Perry. Perry didn't work on her team, but she had worked with him in the past and she liked Perry. He was old school in ways; she understood him and he understood her, but they didn't really talk that much. They were colleagues and would see each other about the station, and when they worked together on the team she never had a problem with him. But it was strange he was calling at this time of night. She picked the phone up, pressed the button, and answered the call.

'Clarissa, sorry,' said Perry. 'Sorry to bother you, um . . . I didn't know who to call, and I'm not sure who's on call at the moment with your lot.'

'It's Patterson, but we're all on a case. What's the matter?' she asked, hearing the serious tone in Perry's voice.

'I'm currently standing on the side of the Cairngorms, and I've got a body.'

'I thought that's what you were meant to do,' said Clarissa.

'Well, I don't go around collecting them,' said Perry suddenly. 'Sorry, but it's got a bracelet on it. I could do with it being identified. Jona's taken a look at it briefly, but she said that she thinks it's, well, it's a collectible, one of your type of things.'

'Collectible? She called it a collectible?'

'No, I called it a collectible,' said Perry. 'She called it a proper antique type thing. I can't remember. Anyway, I've got no ID for the body, yeah? So, I need you or one of your people to come and have a look.'

She thought for a moment. She couldn't send Patterson to that—he wouldn't know, and Sabine was away, back down to Glasgow.

'I'll see the item with Jona in the station. I'll pop by in the morning if that's okay with you, Perry.'

'No,' said Perry. 'Look, I hate to be a pain, but I'd rather you come and have a look at it now.'

'Why?' said Clarissa.

'Well, it's . . . I could do with knowing what it is. Like I say, I've got nowhere to go at the moment. We don't know who the person is, but Jona's going to do DNA and that, but who knows? Fingerprints—they won't necessarily come up with anything. This is the only real tangible thing on the body.'

'Send me a photo,' said Clarissa, and closed down the call. She lay back into Frank, but she was restless now.

'What's up?' he asked.

'I may have to go, Frank. Perry's on the side of the Cairngorms with a body.'

'I thought you didn't do that stuff anymore,' said Frank.

'I don't. It's got a bracelet on it. Jona's said that it's something I should have a look at. Jona doesn't say things lightly. I've asked Perry to send me a photograph. I was going to go in the morning and have a look at it in the station, but he wants me to look at it now.'

'Oh well. Have a look at it then,' said Frank.

Clarissa lay back, her shoulders suddenly feeling tense again. About two minutes later, her phone vibrated, and she quickly took a look at the picture from Perry. The bracelet seemed to be made of bronze and was basic, but it was—wow, she thought—that really looks old. Proper old.

'I'm going to have to go, Frank.'

'I'll wait up for you,' he said.

'No, don't,' she said. 'I don't know what this will be. They'll need me to have a proper look at it.'

'But you're on the other case. You need some sleep.'

'No, I don't. I'm a detective. We run purely on coffee.'

'No, you don't,' said Frank suddenly. 'You don't see Macleod rushing about in the middle of the night.'

'Well, he does, actually. And he also knows it's not good for him. Look, I need to do this. I will get back and get some rest, though, afterwards. Okay? Don't wait up for me. I need you to be on form for me, always.'

'Don't worry about Christmas, either. Don't worry about presents for me.'

'Of course—I hadn't.' Suddenly she was feeling guilty about that.

'I've got the food basically ordered. I can pick it all up, get it all made, yeah? See if you can get back for Christmas dinner at least.'

'I'm going to solve this case before then,' said Clarissa. 'We need our time, Frank, okay? But next time we book time away, we go somewhere. Somewhere Macleod can't haul us back from.'

She found her shawl again, put it on, and gave Frank a wave from the car as she drove out of her own driveway. Heading out towards the Cairngorms in the dead of night, she was amazed as the moon made an appearance. The hills looked alive like they were silver, not just white. There was a beauty at this time of night, a stillness, a cold—a deadly cold, but a beautiful cold.

She worked her way up into the Cairngorms, feeling the little car slip occasionally. There was ice coming now. Had there been a slight melt at some point? It didn't bother her because Clarissa could handle a car, and she drove on until reaching coordinates that Perry had sent through. There she parked up the car, seeing other police, and walked for the best part of a quarter of a mile up into the mountainside.

Perry was waiting for her with a broad smile. The man had a large jacket on, but he looked frozen. He wore flannel trousers underneath and shoes, not boots.

'You need to get wellies and stuff,' said Clarissa. She had large hiking boots on, knowing she was coming up to the mountain, and the shawl and the trousers that she wore were always warm. She had a waterproof set she could put on if needed. But tonight was cold, not wet.

'I can't get the wellies to fit me. I can't be bothered carrying that stuff about. It's not what we ever did. Used to have a cigarette to keep me warm. Not anymore though.'

'Is Hope not coming out?'

'I told her not to.'

'You can't be too protective of her,' said Clarissa. 'You know she's still the boss. She still needs to get about, even though she's pregnant.'

'This is my team,' said Perry in jest. 'I look after mine; you look after yours. Come give me an expert opinion on this.'

'Expert opinion, Detective Inspector?' said Clarissa.

Perry laughed. 'The day you get a rank from me will be the day that—'

Clarissa punched him and walked on. Ahead of her was Jona. She held a coverall suit, and Clarissa asked if it was really necessary for her to put it on.

'I haven't taken the bracelet off the wrist yet. If you want a close-up look, you'll put the full gear on,' said Jona. 'We've put a tent up over there so you can step inside it to change. You need a bit of shelter despite the lack of wind.'

This was true, but Clarissa would have to remove the shawl.

It took her about ten minutes to get herself inside a coverall suit, cover her hair, and when she came out, she could feel the chill. Perry had gone and dressed up too, and the two of them crouched down beside the body.

An arm was stretched out from the male; he was utterly naked. One side of his arm had been under the soil—in fact, most of the body had been.

'What happened?' asked Clarissa.

'Man walking the dog. Dog sniffed something. The man started to dig and then dug a bit more. Found the body. Jona has excavated it more now, after doing all the photos and that. She's going to move it soon, but I think it would have been a while before we got back. I want to get moving on this, see if I can get some idea of who he is before the dust settles.'

'How long's he been in the ground?'

'A couple of days,' said Perry.

'A couple of days?' Clarissa knelt down, looking carefully at the bracelet in front of her. 'Am I okay to touch it?' she asked Jona.

'As long as you've got your gloves on, yes. Take photos around it. Don't take it off the wrist, though.'

'I'm not sure I could get it off the wrist. It's tight, isn't it?'

'That's what I'm thinking,' said Jona. 'He's utterly naked except for that. I don't think they could get it off.'

Clarissa gently turned the bracelet around. It didn't look like much—it was round, but the thickness of it, the colouration . . .

'What are you thinking?' asked Perry.

'See the markings in here, Perry?' Perry was holding the arm up as Clarissa turned the bracelet round.

'Yes,' said Perry.

'This isn't like one of those rheumatic bracelets. This isn't to have copper around your wrist. It's a relic.'

'A relic?'

'Yeah,' said Clarissa. 'This is a Bronze Age bracelet. This may have disappeared three years ago from a Spanish collection.'

'He wouldn't be wearing that if he took it from a collection, would he?'

'No,' said Clarissa. 'You might put it in a collection if money was what you were about. But some of us art collectors, we…, well, I was looking at Cinderella's carriage the other day. The big one.'

'No idea what you're talking about,' said Perry.

'It's a really famous carriage of legend. There were six of them. One small, very small one, and then it goes inside a bigger one, and all the way up until you can fit them all inside the biggest. Anyway, I was beside the biggest, and I'd never seen it before in my life. I got to touch it. For some of us, art is not something to be looked at behind a glass cabinet. It's something to feel, to be near to. It's something to hold on to, Perry. I probably sound like a lunatic, don't I?'

'No,' said Perry. 'I get it.'

'Well, you see, whoever's wearing this is not wearing it because they like a bit of decoration. They're not wearing this because they want to have, like, a diamond on their finger that everybody else will look at. Most people will look at this and not have a clue what it is. This is worn by somebody who really appreciates what it is, who wants to be close to it. Someone who wants to be tactile with it. This is a collector, Perry. I swear this is a collector.'

'Do you know who?'

Clarissa looked down at the face. 'No, but there are plenty

of collectors who are not known by their face, only by their name.'

'So where do I start?' said Perry.

'I don't know,' she said. 'It's going to be awkward. I could try to see if anybody's got a missing collector. Trouble is the whole thing about being quiet and being unavailable, unobtainable—well, if you then go missing, it doesn't really show up, does it?'

'Can you put me in touch with the Spanish authorities, the ones who lost this item?'

'Of course,' said Clarissa. 'I can do that. But the real answer to this is somebody who was tactile to it, somebody who wanted to be with it, wanted it on them because of the history, because of what it was.' She stood up and shivered in the cold.

'How's your case going, anyway?' asked Perry.

'It's a tough one,' she said. 'Moving in a mysterious world at the moment, the underground world of art. The underground collector, the collector that doesn't want to be known. Bit like this fella. 'Anyway, good luck. Got Frank and a warm bed to look forward to.'

'Thanks for your help,' said Perry. 'Send me over those Spanish details. The morning will do for it.'

Clarissa made her way off the hillside in an agitated state. Something was bugging her. Something was kicking at her. She just wasn't sure what.

Chapter 13

Clarissa half wandered, half staggered into the canteen in the Inverness police station the next morning. The time was just after seven. Clarissa felt that she could have gone back to bed instantly. She'd climbed into Frank's arms sometime around three o'clock.

Back in the day, four hours of sleep would have been a luxury. She didn't tell anyone, but in her youth, she was always on the go. Well, she wasn't a harlot, as they would have called her in those days, but she liked to party. And many an early morning she made it back to the house, hoping that her mother wasn't still up. Worse still, her father was standing on the doorstep. These days, getting back in, meant the welcoming arms of Frank.

Unfortunately, she also didn't recover the way she used to.

As she entered the canteen, she saw Patterson tucking into a hearty breakfast. There were sausages, bacon, scrambled egg, a bit of hash browns, as they called them, potato scone. And a hearty cup of black coffee beside him.

'Good morning,' he said, as she half staggered over towards him before plonking herself down on the chair. He shovelled a couple of cuts of sausage into his mouth, swallowed them before he turned to her and said, 'Did you sleep well?'

Clarissa turned her head in complete disbelief. She felt her hand ball into a fist, ready to punch him.

'Did I sleep well? Do I look like someone who's slept well?'

'You don't look any—'

'Stop! Don't say that. Don't even go there. There're times, you know, Pats, you need to learn when to engage the mouth. Sometimes you just need to leave it in neutral and let the brain let that idea slip on past.'

'What was I going to say?'

'You know fine well what you were going to say. Get up there and get me a coffee.'

Patterson stood up, half his breakfast still waiting on the plate. He turned his head in disbelief to Clarissa, saying, 'And sometimes, you need to know when to say please.'

'Please,' said Clarissa, 'but just get me one.'

Patterson walked off and came back with a coffee, placing it in front of her. There was a croissant as well on a small plate. He was good, Patterson.

'What are you so tired for, anyway?' asked Patterson.

'Because, Pats, somebody doesn't know their art yet.' Patterson was bemused. 'I had to go up into the Cairngorms last night. Perry found a body. It had a copper bracelet on it. Proper old one. Ancient. Here, look.'

She took out her phone and showed Patterson a picture. He looked very nonplussed.

'That's from the Bronze Age. That is history. But that is history somebody put on their wrist and somebody else couldn't get that history off their wrist.'

'On a body in the Cairngorms?'

'A naked body. A body that was half buried or attempted to

be buried. But a dog found it and managed to dig it back up. Not that long ago, either. Recent!'

'It's not exactly a very smart-looking item, is it?' said Patterson, looking over the photo of the bracelet again.

'No, it's not, Pats. Somebody wears that because they know their history. They love their art. They love what it is. That bracelet is worth a small fortune, really worth a small fortune. In fact, historically it's worth even more than that.'

'Do you know who it is?' asked Patterson.

'No,' said Clarissa, looking back at her phone as it vibrated in her hand. She saw it was the desk sergeant phoning and switched off the call. Clarissa stood up, drank about half her coffee, stuffed half the croissant in her mouth, and walked off to locate the desk sergeant.

'And what gives you the right to disturb me from my coffee this morning?'

'Got one for you, well, one of your own already,' said the desk sergeant. He was a relatively jolly man, but Clarissa wasn't feeling happy. 'I got a call from one of the units. Katie Grouse has been burgled.'

Clarissa stopped for a moment, looking at him. 'What was taken?'

'A carriage, apparently. Somebody said you'd know about that.'

'You're right, I know about that,' said Clarissa. 'Thanks, George.' She turned and walked away, back into the canteen. Patterson was just finishing his breakfast.

'Katie Grouse has had her carriage burgled.'

'Really?' said Patterson, not looking overly surprised.

'Get the stuff together, and then meet me back here in a couple of minutes.'

'What are you going to do?' asked Patterson.

'As your boss, that's my prerogative, and you don't need to know. But as I'm such a friendly and warm boss, I'll tell you I'm going to finish the rest of this coffee and the other half of the croissant. Get to it.'

Patterson made a mock attempt at running out of the canteen, causing Clarissa to laugh.

She sat down, forced the croissant into her mouth, and then forced it down her throat with some vaguely hot coffee. She sat there taking a moment. Stupid people. You tell them things are being targeted. What do they do about it? Nothing.

Clarissa sighed as she stood back up. She did not need to go to the office—she had everything with her; the shawl was on her; the bag was in the car. She intercepted Patterson coming back into the canteen and together they made it out to the small sports car.

'I hope you're putting the hood up,' said Patterson. 'It's Baltic.'

'Nonsense,' said Clarissa.

She spun the car around and drove out towards the A9 to head for Katie Grouse's. As she did so, the wind whipped through her hair and she felt alive again, woken up by the cool of it. Beside her, Patterson was huddled up, his teeth beginning to chatter.

'You're going to learn to embrace this country,' said Clarissa. 'An old woman like me can go around with this hood down. You need to get a better coat.'

Arriving at Katie Grouse's, Clarissa parked and was taken through by a constable to where Miss Grouse was sitting in her office.

'So you've got here! Have you any word on it? Do you know who has it?'

'Excuse me, Miss Grouse, but I'll need to ask you a few things about the—'

'The theft? You need to ask me? I need to ask you! What are you doing about it? How are you going about finding it?'

'That's not how this works,' said Clarissa. She gave a nod to Patterson, who wandered off. 'May I suggest that leaving the artefact where it was, wasn't the best of options? Plenty of security available. I don't see why you couldn't have used it. You didn't even put it in the secure room.'

'What is the point of having something that you want to look at if you can't look at it? Besides, this is my home they invaded. My home they came into!'

'Are we aware of how they got in?' asked Clarissa.

'How they got in? How do you think they got in? They got in through the back door. Back door was bloody well open.'

'Excuse me?' said Clarissa. 'The back door was open?'

At this point, she noticed that a sergeant was in the room's corner. He seemed to busy himself, but Clarissa called over to him.

'Can I get an update?' she said.

'Of course, Detective Inspector,' said the sergeant. He went to take Clarissa to one side, but Katie Grouse followed them.

'I can hear this too,' she said.

Clarissa stopped for a moment, thought about it, and then gave a nod to the sergeant.

'Well, Inspector, when we arrived, the rear door was open into the room that was housing the carriage. From footprints in the snow, or at least disturbance in the snow, it looks like they came in through the garden.'

'Early hours of the morning, though,' said Katie. 'The door was locked.'

'The door was open when we got here,' said the sergeant. 'If I may, it's a basic locking mechanism. I could break that open.'

'You said about disturbances in the snow,' said Clarissa.

'You'll need to get forensics onto it,' said Katie Grouse.

'We could do, but to be honest,' said the sergeant, 'as far as I can make out, the only footprints out there seem to be that of Miss Grouse and her staff. The other footprints that would have been there were covered in, as the person backtracked away. At least that's how I read it. Forensics can obviously update you on that.'

'So what are you telling me?' asked Clarissa. 'They jumped over the back fence, wandered up, came through that door and then came back out? Any CCTV?'

'Yes. But all it shows is a black figure coming in and going out again. We could probably get an approximate height from it, but I'm not sure it's going to reveal a lot. I'm no expert in this CCTV analysis, but it looks to me like they've got a lot of padding on.'

'You'll have to take me to see it,' said Clarissa.

'This way,' said the sergeant.

'I'm coming too,' said Grouse.

Clarissa was led through to where the CCTV was played back. The sergeant was right. The infiltrator, all dressed in black, looked to have parts of the body that were enlarged, padding added. Trying to get a sense of their figure was difficult. That and the fact that the CCTV was operating in the dark.

'You see their gait too,' said the sergeant. 'That's forced. That's not how that person walks.'

'Whoever's doing it isn't an idiot,' said Clarissa.

'Of course, they're not an idiot. They came in and they stole my carriage,' said Grouse. 'Now what are you going to do about it?'

Clarissa was having an awful morning. The lack of sleep didn't help, and she whirled around, the shawl flying.

'We had two thefts reported to us,' said Clarissa. 'I came, and I told you that these items were highly sought after. I said there was a possibility that someone would come. You left your carriage out in the open, not in your strong room, at a back door that anyone can break into. Quite frankly, I don't know what you expect from me.'

'I expect you to get it back,' said the woman abruptly.

'We're not in your business now. I'm not your junior executive,' said Clarissa. 'I'm Detective Inspector Clarissa Urquhart. And you did not heed my warning. I'll sort this out, but you need to understand that this is missing because of what you did and your actions. Now reel yourself in, woman!'

Clarissa realised she had overstepped the mark with the 'reel yourself in' comment, and this was substantiated by the look on the sergeant's face. He was almost drawing away from the two women as she said it.

'You don't get to speak to me like that!'

'I'll speak to you whatever way I want to when you've been this foolish,' said Clarissa. Even as she said it, she realised Macleod would not be happy.

'If I may,' said a voice. There was Patterson entering the room. 'I've just been to talk to one of the constables. He said that—'

'Don't interrupt! I'm talking to your inspector.'

Patterson stopped for a moment. Surely he could see the steam rising from the two women.

'My constable is coming to talk to me. He may have

something useful. Kindly shush.'

'You can't shush me—'

'Miss Grouse,' said Patterson, raising his voice. 'May I ask, is our officer correct saying that you had a flasher in recent weeks?'

'What on earth's that got to do with it?'

'You had a flasher in the rear garden of your house?'

'Well, yes! Yes,' she said. 'I did.'

'What did they look like?' asked Clarissa suddenly.

'What do you mean, "what do they look like?"'

'Shape, size, details,' said Clarissa, and then stopped suddenly, realising that wasn't the best way to phrase it.

'Other people have had flashers,' said Patterson. 'We need to know the rough height of the person. Hair colour. That sort of thing. Physique.'

'Brown hair. Brown-haired man. I didn't see much of the physique. Large coat on. They were moving away from the house when they turned.'

'So how do you not know the physique?' said Clarissa.

'Because they turned and lifted their coat and showed me their bottom.'

Clarissa wasn't sure this was technically flashing. Possibly it was, but not in the traditional sense.

'What was their bottom like?' asked Clarissa.

'What do you mean, "what was their bottom like?" It was a bottom. It had two cheeks.'

'Was there any hair?' asked Patterson.

'What?'

'You'd have seen the legs, seen the thighs. You'd have seen the buttocks. Maybe you'd have seen the top of the back. Was there any hair? Was it a hairy man?'

'No, it was . . . well, a man that wasn't that well-built, more trim, more petite. No hair I saw.'

Patterson made a note of this in his pocketbook.

'That's interesting,' said Clarissa.

'Why are you interested in a flasher? Why are you interested in somebody who's here to sexually harass me when I reported a theft?'

'You've just been burgled,' said Clarissa. 'People scope out houses. Maybe he wasn't intending to flash you, maybe he was scoping the house. You caught him, and he improvised. Quite interesting, clever really.'

'Clever? What is this?' said Grouse. 'I want my carriage back!'

'Well, hopefully they haven't melted it down or something,' said Clarissa.

She was being mischievous now. There was no way that carriage was being melted down. It wouldn't be worth what it could garner made up.

'If you'll excuse me,' said Clarissa. 'I'll try to find it for you. Come on, Pats. Time to recover what somebody's misplaced.'

Clarissa strode off, determined not to look back. Macleod had spoken to her before about dealing with either suspects or victims. Well, the woman had it coming to her. She went for Clarissa, and there was no way she was ever going to ignore that kind of barbed attack.

Chapter 14

Sabine Ferguson knocked on the door of Emmett's flat. It was about ten seconds later when the door opened and Emmett stood there in a t-shirt and jeans. The t-shirt had what could only be described as a scantily dressed witch, holding the head of someone. It wasn't erotic. It was striking though, and rather a contrast to the demure man who wore it.

'What on earth's that?' said Sabine, pointing at the t-shirt.

'Good, isn't it?' said Emmett. 'She's a witch. Not a nice witch, either. Come on in. I'm just about ready.'

'You think we'll be going back up the road?' said Sabine. 'Everything seems to be quite dead here at the moment.'

'Well, I don't know,' said Emmett. 'You and Clarissa are the ones who know the contacts around here. Is there anywhere else we can try?'

'We've gone through most of them.'

'I expect we'll hear from her soon, anyway.'

Sabine had followed Emmett up the stairs to his flat. Once inside, she sat down on the sofa. She'd been here a few times, and sure enough, on the main table in the living room was a set of miniatures being painted. By the looks of it, he was halfway through them, having deployed a base colour.

'You doing these last night?'

'Did an hour when I came in,' said Emmett. 'It helps you nod off before you go to bed, you know?'

Sabine looked over. There were shelves on the far side of the living room. On them were dragons, space marines, all sorts of fantasy figures that Emmett had painted up. It was like being in one of those shops that catered for the gaming community.

Emmett disappeared for about five minutes and then came back. He had clearly just washed his face. He now had a plain t-shirt on, as well as a pair of black jeans, and was wearing hiking boots.

'Well, I've not heard from her, so I guess we'll make the trip back up. You got your bag ready?'

'Bag's always ready,' said Emmett. 'You never know when she's going to leap us into action.'

Sabine stood up and felt the vibration of her phone. She took it out of her pocket and answered the call.

'Where are the two of you?'

'Well, good morning to you, boss,' said Sabine. 'We're still in Glasgow, just about to head up the road. Found nothing out. Nobody's gone near any of this. It's not happening. Haulage didn't touch any of it. In fact, Haulage was scared off. Garrick's the problem. No one wants to touch it.'

'Well, if the likes of Haulage won't touch it, maybe . . . hang on a minute,' said Clarissa.

Sabine stood with the phone to her ear. It wasn't uncommon that Clarissa would just make you hang during a call because she wanted to look at something. Emmett was using his hands to gesticulate 'are we coming or going?' but Sabine shrugged her shoulders.

'Is Stores about?'

'Stores?' said Sabine. 'Stores doesn't usually get involved with the likes of—'

'The likes of this. This is high class. Stores might be involved in it. I know she's not round Glasgow, but I did hear a rumour that she had been doing some trailing.'

'I'll check it out,' said Sabine.

'See if she knows anything. Then, if not, I'll think about getting you back up here.'

Sabine closed the call then and looked at Emmett. 'She wants us to check out Stores.'

'Which stores?' asked Emmett.

'No, no. It's not a shop. It's a person. Michelle "Stores" Killarney. Irish woman. Sometimes does business in Glasgow. I get where Clarissa's coming from. She's high end in the market. Not necessarily thinking it would be her sort of thing, but if Garrick's a threat and you need it moved quietly, you need someone special. Stores could do it. Stores can be very secretive. I wonder if she's about?'

Sabine picked up the phone again and dialled a number. 'Best get a coffee, Emmett. Me too. I'm going to be a while on this one.'

Emmett came back and placed a coffee down in front of Sabine while he went off to paint again. It was an hour and a half on phone calls to ten different people before Sabine had tracked down Michelle Killarney.

'She's meeting a dealer in a wine bar. It's all above ground, this meeting. But I think we can bump in, catch her while she's there.'

'What sort of person is she?'

'She's class,' said Sabine. 'She'll know that we know she deals in illegal items. And she'll also know that we can't get her for any of it at the moment. She won't tell you anything that will implicate herself but she may be quite open about this. We'll see. Anyway, put that paintbrush down. Let's get going.'

The wine bar was in the middle of Glasgow and quite unusual. As they approached it, it was just past twelve, and the wine bar was open for lunch.

Sabine stopped Emmett at the door, pointing down to the far end of the bar. There was a woman there in black trousers, with long red hair, and a rather daring looking top.

'Is that her?'

'She's twenty-seven,' said Sabine. 'She's twenty-seven, and she operates on the top of this game.'

'Impressive.'

The pair walked in and slowly made their way down the bar. There was a glance at them from Michelle Killarney, but little else. Sabine pulled a chair up beside Killarney, and Emmett stood on the other side.

'Well,' said Killarney, 'if it isn't my favourite sergeant. How are you?'

'Very well,' said Sabine. 'Been a while since I saw you.'

'Been a while since I was in Glasgow. A few other things on the go. Decent jobs elsewhere. Still, giving your head peace for a while, eh?'

Sabine smiled. 'I bet you've heard?'

'Heard?'

'Cinderella carriages.'

'Absolutely. But before I say anything, who's this rather lovely young man you've got with you?' asked Michelle.

'I think you're young to be describing me as young,' said

Emmett.

'Well, I'm not bothered about age,' said Michelle. 'I am bothered when I don't know who someone is.'

'This is Detective Sergeant Emmett Grump.'

'Oh, the new one with you! I'd heard that someone said you were about with somebody different. You an art lover, Emmett?' said Killarney.

'Not overly. Brought on for my detective work.'

'That's a pity. You can sometimes blind the arts ones.'

'Cinderella carriages,' said Sabine. 'You heard much about them?'

'Heard about them? They're the worst kept secret going, but that's probably because one of them got stolen from Garrick.'

'Have you worked for Garrick before?'

'Garrick and I have had reason occasionally to join forces to acquire, obviously in a reputable way, certain items.'

'You didn't acquire the carriage for him originally, did you?' asked Sabine.

'He's had it for a while,' said Michelle.

'Awkward items to be taken, aren't they, though?' said Sabine.

'Well, we've seen two of them disappear, haven't we?'

'Three,' said Sabine. 'One taken last night.'

'And you're here to see me? I don't move that quickly. Where was the other one taken from?'

'Inverness area.'

'Well, that's not out yet. Hasn't hit the grapevine. Probably will by the end of today, if you lot know it.'

'Are you involved?'

Michelle shook her head, the red hair fanning out behind her.

'Tell me, Emmett,' said Michelle, 'do you know how things are moved about? Moved about illegally?'

'Well, usually someone takes it on board to move it for the eventual owner,' said Emmett. 'Someone with a bit of influence. Someone who can hide it away. Move it without it being seen. They'll have a network of people they can call upon.'

'Do you know what these people look like?' said Michelle.

'Well, some of them look like Haulage. But others work in classier establishments.'

'Some of them do,' said Michelle. 'And some of them are wiser than the likes of Haulage. It takes a certain type of person on this. Haulage would run from it because Garrick's involved.'

'Haulage said as much,' said Sabine. 'Said he wouldn't go near it because of Garrick.'

'Garrick would kill him,' said Michelle quietly. 'Mr Garrick's reputation of quick brutality is a threat to take seriously. He doesn't take kindly to being double-crossed. He doesn't take kindly to people that steal his stuff. I haven't had occasion to cross Garrick. I'm not stupid. If I move things, I know where they've come from. I know where they're going. And if the person receiving them isn't able to take care of the person you've taken it from, well, you have second thoughts and you need certain insurances put in place. However, I am someone capable of that. I put out some feelers.'

'For the carriages?'

'Yes. You ever seen them?' she said to Sabine.

'Saw one recently,' said Sabine, 'up in Inverness, but it's disappeared.'

'What was it like?' She sat forward, almost eager, like a schoolchild.

'Exquisite,' said Sabine. 'The whole feel of it, the look of it, like a fairy tale made real.'

'I'll be honest with you,' said Michelle. 'You and I stand on separate sides at times, but with this one, there's nothing for us to be on separate sides for. I put out feelers to try to see if anyone was looking for the items to be moved, but I heard nothing back.'

'So, someone was using someone else?'

'No,' said Michelle. 'I don't believe so. I wanted to get these items in transit, because at some point I wanted to see them. Feel them, touch them, hold them for an hour or two. They are, well, as you know, almost legend. But very real legend.'

'Are you saying that nobody is moving these?' asked Sabine.

'You know, I'm saying no one seems to know who has the items. Garrick's the victim, so whoever has them may be holding them tight because they know Garrick will come for them if it's on the grapevine. That causes a problem, though.'

'Which is?' asked Emmett.

'If nobody knows about them, if you hold them tight,' said Sabine, 'you can't ship them on. You can't get a price from them, you can't get them away to the person they were meant to go to. A collector wouldn't take them in person, you'd make sure it came from a third party. You wouldn't contact each other, not with something of this value. So, they could be in for the long haul. They may store it away for a year, two years. Maybe gather them all, then hand them over a couple of years' time.'

'Because a true collector—'

'A true collector wouldn't mind that,' said Michelle, 'as long as you had it in the end.'

'Of course, there's the other side of it,' said Emmett.

'Which is?' asked Michelle.

'The person who took it wanted it for themselves. People that own these things—'

Michelle interrupted. 'People that own these things or who want to own them, they don't get their hands dirty in that way. People work through an intermediate because then if the person procuring it gets arrested, you're not sullied. You need somebody high-class, and you need somebody who is expendable.

'I personally don't believe myself to be expendable, but those who hire me do, and I would not give up where I was putting an item. It's part of the deal, and there's no paperwork anyway, so it doesn't matter. They can't pin it on anyone else, just you, but it rewards you well.'

Michelle turned and smiled. 'So you see, it's probably as Sabine and I described it.'

'Only if you want it because you want the items for bragging rights, or for moving it on and selling.'

'Well, why else would you want them?' said Michelle. 'It's art, it's classic, wonderful items.'

'I don't know,' said Emmett, 'but I can't believe it. I can't believe those are the only reasons you'd ever steal anything.'

Sabine called the bartender over, handed him over a fiver, and told him to get a drink for the lady next to her.

'We'll see you around,' said Sabine, as she and Emmett turned away from Michelle.

'You're looking well,' Michelle said to Sabine. 'Always nicer to see you than the other one. Oh, and very cute!' She smiled at Emmett.

As they walked out the door, Sabine said to Emmett, 'Don't worry. She treats all men like that.'

'I wasn't complaining,' said Emmett. 'Besides, I think she's missing something.'

'What?' said Sabine.

'Not everybody loves art. Not everyone's a fan.'

Chapter 15

The Cairngorms and the bracelet on the body were on Clarissa's mind. Who would have that bracelet there? Who was the man? It didn't matter how much her own current case was getting in the way, part of her couldn't help but think about it. She wandered along the corridor, stopped, and stood looking down at Perry.

He was dressed as usual in a suit that looked like it had been thrown on to him, and he stood there almost impassive, by the smokers' shelter. The great wheels of his mind would be turning over because that's how Perry worked. Part of Clarissa wanted to be on that case because she wanted to know where that bracelet had come from, whose it was. It had a story to tell, and that was half of the joy with the art world—stories. Cinderella's carriage had intrigued her too, but she was still smarting from speaking to Katie Grouse that morning. The woman was ignorant, completely ignorant. Snap her fingers. Do this, do that.

How did somebody like that get hold of such a wonderful item and then not look after it? Clarissa must have been tired because she was getting agitated with nobody around her. Agitated at somebody's negligence of an item that Clarissa didn't even own. Art items went on the move all the time—people stealing them, people buying them back. This wasn't uncommon in the art world. Maybe she should see about that bracelet, though. She could be of use. Perry would be no good to them. He wouldn't understand it. Sabine, yes, she could do it, but Sabine was Glasgow-based.

Clarissa would have time, wouldn't she? She could take it on top of her current case. Clarissa found herself walking the stairs up to Macleod's office. She looked over at the secretary on the desk outside and shouted over to her, 'Is he in with anyone?'

The woman shook her head, went to pick up the phone to announce Clarissa's arrival, but Clarissa was already at the door. She thundered on it with her fist before opening it. As she stepped in, she saw Macleod looking out the window.

'There's no need to knock if you're just going to barge in,' he said. 'The idea of knocking is so I can say whether it's appropriate to come in.'

'Your secretary said you weren't in with anyone.'

'I could have been getting changed,' said Macleod.

He hadn't turned round; he was still looking out the window.

'Getting changed?' said Clarissa. 'Why would you ever get changed in here? Anyway, listen up—'

'I'm sorry?' said Macleod.

'Listen, Seoras, you know the case that Hope's on—'

'Oh, you're talking about the body. Good of you to go out last night. Perry said you were quite tired. So good of you to get on to it. I think they're going in the right direction with it.'

'That bracelet—it's quite something. I think it could be a line of attack to go down. I'm quite happy to jump on board for a day or two.'

'It's fine,' said Macleod.

'What do you mean, "It's fine"? Perry said that he needed to identify the man and he hasn't yet.'

'No, he hasn't,' said Macleod flatly.

'Well, I'll jump on board with him. I can help him with that.'

'You have a case at the moment.' Still, Macleod hadn't turned round. Clarissa was getting annoyed with him.

'I can handle the case. There's four of us. We're on it. I've got the gang down in Glasgow running through leads.'

'So what do we have?' said Macleod, his back still to her.

'Would you turn round, Man? For goodness sake.'

Slowly, Macleod turned round. 'Remind me,' he said, 'to tell Perry to get somebody else out in the middle of the night. Because somebody needs their sleep.'

'Piss off, Seoras,' she said.

'You had a problem today. Something up?'

'I'm not going to apologise. You've stood with your back to me for how long?'

'You barged into my room. What did you expect?' he said.

'Seoras, this bracelet, I can help with that. I can—'

'It's fine.'

'No, it's not,' said Clarissa. 'I was out last night because you needed someone who could identify it. Patterson wouldn't have had a clue. But I saw it, I had a good idea what it was, and then I verified it. That's my expertise. You needed me on this case to help Perry, to help Hope.'

'It's Hope's. If Hope requires help, Hope will ask for it. Okay! At the moment, the Chief Constable wants you on these carriages. And I believe we've actually lost another one.'

'We didn't lose another one,' said Clarissa. 'That clown, Katie Grouse, lost another one.'

'Let's not refer to our victims as clowns,' said Macleod. 'It comes out in press conferences when you don't mean it to. Besides, she's not a clown.'

'She is a clown. We were there. Sabine went. She told her about the others being stolen. And yet the woman leaves it in a living room.'

'She's entitled to.'

'And then she's entitled to get it nicked. She had a strong room, Seoras. Do you know that? She had a strong room. If she had used the room, it would have been difficult to get. But no. She said she wanted it there because she wanted to look at it.'

'Does she know the price of it?' asked Macleod.

'She must do. Anyway, they're priceless. You can't get a proper value on them. You can't. Anyway, I was wondering—'

'No,' said Macleod. 'You can't go on to Hope's case.'

Clarissa went to speak, but there was a rap on the door.

'Now that's a rap. That's not a "I am coming in anyway" rap,' said Macleod. 'That's one of two people because it's incredibly polite. That's either Ross or it's Patterson. Now, Ross, I believe, is currently out dealing with that case, so this will be Patterson. Come in, Eric,' said Macleod, raising his voice.

The door opened slowly. Patterson stepped in and closed the door behind him and then wandered forward.

'Excuse me, Seoras. I need to speak to Clarissa.'

'What?' said Clarissa, agitated.

'It's to do with the case. I've been going through the backgrounds of our victims, our carriage owners. Lady Angela and Katie—they're related.'

'What do you mean "they're related"?'

'Katie Grouse and Lady Angela McPhail are related. They're

sisters. Katie's the older sister. Angela is forty, Katie's forty-three.'

'You're joking,' said Clarissa.

'No, I'm not,' he said. 'I'm trying to see what other families are around them, but it's not that clear. I'm going through records.'

'Very good,' said Clarissa. She said this because Macleod was there, and she saw Patterson roll his eyes. He knew where the compliment was coming from. 'I'll speak to you later,' said Clarissa. Patterson gave a nod to Macleod and left the room.

'Hope needs me in this case. If you're going to find out who this guy is, you need me!'

'If Hope wants you,' reiterated Macleod, 'Hope will request you. I am not putting you on that case. And if she does, I'll pull Sabine over to help her. You need to get on to your case and you need to get it solved. Chief Constable is on my back the whole time about it. I'm keeping him out of your way, but you need to get something for me. You need to get results.'

'I can cover both,' said Clarissa.

'I didn't make heads of each team so the head of the team could run into another team all the time.'

'Well, I had to get pulled out last night, didn't I?' she said. 'You can't pull me into an investigation and then walk me out again.'

'I can,' said Macleod. 'And besides, I didn't pull you in. Perry did. I've asked Perry next time to request Sabine or one of the others.'

'No, you don't,' said Clarissa. 'That's my call.'

'And you called it by legging it out there yourself. You're barely getting enough sleep with this case as it is. It's full on. We need to get on top of it and we need to solve it quick. That's fine. I don't mind you working through the midnight hours on that. But you don't jump on to another case.'

'Sabine wasn't about. It's a dead body; it's—'

'Not more important than your cases,' said Macleod. 'I've said no. Now go find these carriages.'

Clarissa almost shook her fist. She didn't, but turned and stopped herself from slamming the door behind her. Maybe he was right. But no. Trouble with the arts world was if you weren't in it, you didn't get it. And they needed an expert. And you didn't want an expert who was from a university about these things. You needed a detective. You needed someone who could put the nastier implications around an item.

Clarissa marched down the stairs into her office and sat down. Patterson, at the other end of the small office, had his head down behind the computer screen and was not raising it back up. *He can sense the mood*, she thought. 'Stuff this,' she said to herself. She stood up and marched out of her office, round to the Murder Squad's larger office. Hope was in her own small office adjacent to it.

Clarissa knocked on the door, almost politely, before being told to come in. She gently closed the door behind her.

'How are you doing?' asked Clarissa.

'I'm fine. Sick of everybody asking me how I'm doing. I'm pregnant, not ill.'

'Sorry,' said Clarissa. 'I was just being polite. Never been pregnant so I haven't got a clue what it's like.'

'Don't mind me,' said Hope. 'Just a little—well, I came back after being away with John for a bit. Macleod's idea. And it was good. I loved it.'

'I'm sorry,' said Clarissa.

'I can't stay away when murder cases are on like this. I'm

going to be out of action later on in this pregnancy and after the wee one's born.'

'I was out last night,' said Clarissa, 'looking at that bracelet on the victim's body.'

'Yes, Perry said. Sorry to get you out. He didn't go through me. He just rang you straight. But Macleod said I'm to leave you alone.'

'I know he doesn't want us beholden to each other. He doesn't want us working across because we're at the top of the teams. But Sabine's in Glasgow. She's working on something for me. But you need someone on this bracelet.'

'How?' asked Hope.

'The bracelet. As I said to Perry, that's an expensive bracelet. That's a bracelet that most collectors would stick in a strong room. You would keep it away, take it out occasionally to look at. You do not wear a bracelet like that around your wrist, especially when it's that tight. That bracelet's not coming off. That person is, as I said, tactile. They needed contact with that bracelet. It means something more to them. It is someone with a passion for the art. Real passion.'

'Okay,' said Hope. 'How's that helping me?'

'Well, your man will be heavily into the art world, but also he's got to have obtained it at some point. Something like that ends up in a museum. It's Bronze Age—history. It's not just a delightful piece of art that's been done in the last couple of hundred years. Actual history. If he's obtained it, he's probably done it by, well, not necessarily strictly legal means. If you can trace the bracelet, if you can trace those movements, you might trace who he is. I assume you still haven't identified him?'

'I can't get a match on him at all. Dental records, DNA,

nothing is coming up to identify this person. It's like they're a ghost.'

'And that's why they're in the art world. They're one of the secret collectors, they're one of the people who works behind everything. They'll have a lot of money.'

'But don't you know them then?'

'A lot of these people are faceless,' Clarissa said. 'Some of them are just names you don't get to meet. So, what do you say? Deal with me on this, okay? Seoras won't let me run off and do it. If I do that, he'll kick me out of the job. He's basically told me I'm to do my case. Chief Constable's all over it. I know I can charge in and whatever, but if I do that in this instance and I go off and investigate your case, I'll be up for it. You'll be in it as well. It won't work. He's put the foot down. But deal with me on it directly. Keep telling me what you find out.'

'So you're saying what? You want us to do the spade work?'

'Yes. That's it,' said Clarissa. 'Talk to me, but do the spade work. You're going to have to deal with some people that are not your normal people either. You're going to have to be discreet, and you're going to have to know when to push. Take Perry with you.'

'Why Perry?' asked Hope.

'Susan's a lovely girl, very with it, very astute. But she's green around the edges with playing the darker areas. Perry is not an idiot. Perry is very clever and Perry knows when to push and when not to. He'll think before jumping in. As much as you think I don't, when it comes to my world, I do. And Perry will pick up and act on it correctly. And he'll keep you from going so by the book that you blow it.'

'Well, thanks for that,' said Hope. 'If ever there's a compliment—'

'I'm being serious,' said Clarissa suddenly. 'My world's a bit more shadowy. You can't go by the book at times. And you can't with this or you'll never find him. Have you got a pad of paper?'

Hope handed the pad of paper over to Clarissa. Clarissa wrote a name and an address.

'Go here, speak to this person. They might know about it. They'll hopefully be able to direct you on the right path. Drop my name. But beware in case they run. And then tell me how you got on.'

Clarissa turned on her heel and went to walk out the door, but Hope called her back. 'Wait a minute,' she said, as Clarissa turned back. 'Thanks.'

'It's fine,' said Clarissa. 'We've got to know when to work together. Sometimes you have to manage your boss.'

She turned back and walked out the door. It sounded good—manage your boss—but what had actually happened was Clarissa had gone and helped Hope without actually getting on to the case herself. Macleod had once again played her. One day she was going to go up there, and she was going to slap him. She was getting used to this—Macleod playing her, getting what he needed, getting it done how he wanted it.

Still, she thought, *time to get back to the carriages*.

Chapter 16

Clarissa sat in her office as Patterson pulled a chair up beside her. Her laptop was on, and she was awaiting the call from Sabine and Emmett to pull everyone together and decide what to do next. Patterson had put the coffee down at the end of the table and Clarissa was drinking it. It was strong, and it needed to be, because she was shattered. Being out last night hadn't helped in the slightest. However, she was now focused on her carriages, part of her happy that she'd got involved with Hope's case.

'Where are they?' asked Patterson.

'She was going to pull in, try to find somewhere to do the conference from. They've been out in the car.'

'Oh well, that's good,' said Patterson. 'Did they give a time?'

'They'll be on, Pats,' said Clarissa. 'It's not Macleod doing this; it's me, okay? I know how to operate technology, albeit not as good as you.'

'Just saying, because if they're going to be ten or fifteen minutes, I've stuff I can do.'

'Pats, sit, shush. If we get five, ten, fifteen minutes, relax, have a rest, all right? Recharge those batteries.'

Clarissa sat back and let out a yawn. She ignored Patterson's stare at her. There was a beep from the computer, and she saw Sabine was calling in. She pressed the button and saw the picture expand. On the screen in front of her was Sabine and Emmett, both with earphones on.

'Are you somewhere secure?'

'Outside a cafe. It's blooming cold, but it was too noisy inside. Also too many ears. We're good to chat here, though.'

'Excellent,' said Clarissa. 'Right, what have you got for me?'

'We found Stores,' said Sabine. 'But it's unlikely the collection's being stolen for money. Stores says that there's nothing. I can't believe that Haulage and Stores have both looked to get a reaction on moving the carriages, and both of them are coming up saying it's quiet. They can't be being moved.'

'What does that mean?' asked Patterson.

'It means,' said Clarissa, 'it's either a specific collector it's been done for, in which case they may even hold the items for a year or two before shipping them on. This would get them cover and make sure that Garrick doesn't come after them. Or it's someone quiet and—'

'Or it could mean,' said Emmett, 'that the person stealing them is the one that's going to have them.'

'But why?' asked Clarissa. 'People who obtain these things, they don't steal personally. They're collectors; they keep their noses clean by using that intermediary. And then if it turns up, oh mysteriously, paperwork arrives from a secret auction from somebody or somewhere if they ever have to show how they got the item. In any case, they'll never have stolen it. There'll be no transaction to say they've stolen it; therefore, we can't pin them. All we can do is take the item back off them because they bought it in good faith. There'll be a money receipt somewhere, although it won't be produced until asked for.'

'Complicated, this art world, isn't it?' said Patterson.

'Pats has also discovered Lady Angela and our friend Katie Grouse are sisters,' said Clarissa.

'Really?' said Emmett. 'That's interesting.'

'Why?' asked Clarissa.

'They just have three out of the six carriages. Where'd they come from? What money? How'd they get them?'

'Well, Lady Angela got hers before she married her husband in a secret auction,' said Clarissa.

'Secret auction. Everybody says secret auction,' said Emmett suddenly. 'What on earth is a secret auction?'

'Does what it says on the tin,' said Clarissa. 'I know you're not au fait with the art world and the way things happen, but secret auction for somebody who has an item means they can contact certain people. It's not held publicly, so bids are made by whatever method, and then the winner gets it, and they get a receipt. So it's legitimate, but it's behind closed doors.'

'And how did these people afford such items? How was that done?' asked Emmett.

'Maybe the person didn't know the value of them,' said Clarissa.

'And yet they ran a secret auction,' said Sabine.

'Something's not sitting, is it?' said Emmett.

'One of the problems, Emmett, is that things don't look like they sit,' said Clarissa. 'And Sabine will tell you this, because people don't give out much information. Got to be careful in this world that you don't read too much into things.'

'She has a point there,' said Sabine to Emmett, 'but you have a point too. I don't think we should write Emmett's points off the board.'

'Absolutely not,' said Clarissa. 'But what do we do? How do we move on from here?'

'Well, I'm still dirt digging,' said Patterson.

'Great,' said Clarissa, as if the comment meant nothing. 'I also have to tell you I've been engaging with Hope about the dead man on the hillside. They're going to go off and do a bit of digging for us.'

'Why do you say that?' said Emmett. 'Has he got anything to do with this case?'

'No, I've no evidence of that. But, think about it. They've suddenly got a dead body with an incredibly ostentatious and expensive piece of art on their wrist. One that can't be removed. The man's dead; he's naked and buried. That's a collector, a really significant collector. Someone who loves their art. That's someone that wants to be part of the art. It's not somebody that's in it just for the money.

'We now have items not being moved. You've brought up, Emmett, that it may be for reasons other than financial or for simply having it as your possession. I know it's tenuous, but is there a link there between that and the dead man?'

'Fair play,' said Emmett. 'Keep it out there. Keep it in the open. At least you're talking to Hope about it, so you'll get plenty of feedback on that one.'

'It doesn't help us though. Chief Constable is still jumping up and down, still wants things solved. So how do we go about this? We can't trap the stolen carriages on the move. We've no idea where the last three items have gone.'

'We've got a Peeping Tom,' said Patterson.

'Peeping Tom?' said Emmett. 'Another one?'

'Yes,' said Clarissa. 'Patterson discovered that Lady Angela has been receiving a Peeping Tom as well. She got flashed.'

'So we've got a description of him,' said Emmett.

'No,' said Patterson. 'We've got a description of his backside. Apparently non-hairy, toned figure.'

'So we've got a Peeping Tom at Lady Angela's. There's been a Peeping Tom at Katie Grouse's,' said Emmett. 'Neither of them have been flashed in a conventional sense. And you're now telling me that Lady Angela's one . . . well, how did you put it?'

'Didn't have a hairy arse,' said Clarissa. Patterson rolled his eyes at her.

'Didn't have a hairy arse,' repeated Emmett. 'Peeping Tom. Doesn't sound like a man, does it?'

'What do you mean?' asked Clarissa. 'The flasher's a woman? You're telling me what, I've got a lesbian flasher on the go?'

'If you're a Peeping Tom, or if you're a flasher, as a man to a woman, what's the one thing you're trying to do?'

'Oh, you're trying to shock them by showing your what, dingle-dangle,' said Sabine.

'Your dingle-dangle,' laughed Clarissa.

'Well, she's right,' said Emmett. 'Your dingle-dangle. The dingle-dangle has not been shown. Why?'

Clarissa put her hand down on the table and then shook her head. 'I was out on the side of the Cairngorms last night and I'm sitting now in a meeting talking about why a flasher doesn't show their dingle-dangle. I hope this is relevant.'

'It's very relevant,' said Emmett, with no sense of amusement. 'I'm just not sure how, but both places have had the carriages nicked.'

'We couldn't get any footprints either,' said Patterson, 'from this one, because they were blotted out in the snow. The forensic team have come back and said there are no decent footprints. All the footprints are from the staff. Or from Katie Grouse.'

'So they're sisters,' said Emmett. 'They've both had Peeping Toms, and both have been flashed badly.'

'A lot of bizarre connections,' said Sabine. 'Neither of them seems to appreciate the carriages either. Certainly not their value. They're not stored away, they're not locked. Our first two thefts—'

'Don't tell me they don't seem to appreciate them,' said Clarissa. 'I disagree with that. Garrick would have known exactly, but Garrick tried to protect it by anonymity. Ursula Knight would have known as well; she had security systems— they just were breached.'

'Lady Angela's are well covered too,' said Patterson, 'but she's taking them tonight to her friends.'

'You'd think you'd protect them better, wouldn't you?' said Clarissa.

'That's why Sabine's on to something,' said Emmett. 'How do you not know the value of these? You know them, Clarissa. I wouldn't,' said Emmett. 'You know it because you're in the world. You see the value monetarily, in the sense that they struggle to value them, they're so expensive. You see the value of them in terms of their exquisiteness. Do either Katie Grouse or Lady Angela see that? How was Katie Grouse when they were taken?'

'Seemed more annoyed,' said Patterson, 'that somebody got into her house. She wants her carriage back. She seems offended by the fact it's happened to her. Now that's not unusual when people get robbed. Seeing your own house, your privacy taken away, that sense of invulnerability lost, that sense of losing a place to rest.'

'But what about the item?' said Emmett. 'Did she appreciate the item? The loss?'

'No,' said Clarissa. 'She was raging at me, but not in that way. There was no mournfulness for it. There was no deep regret, like you had your child taken from you.'

'Why would there be?' said Patterson.

'And that's the point,' said Emmett. 'See, Patterson doesn't get it. He doesn't get that mournfulness you're talking about. He's not a collector. Patterson's not a real art person. Is Lady Angela? I'm not so sure. She's taking her babies to a soiree. We've got the big coach going on a parade. These are not real art people, and yet, you tell me they've gone to a secret auction.'

Emmett was quite agitated now, almost emotional, in a way Clarissa hadn't seen him.

'What are you saying?'

'Clarissa, there's a story here. There's a story here we're not seeing.'

'Well get yourselves back up the road,' said Clarissa, 'because we need to get after this. I don't know how.'

'We've got to become more proactive,' said Emmett suddenly. 'Somebody's coming for these items, and we need to be there with them. Tonight—somebody needs to be there. There are only three carriages left and two of them are being put out, not quite in the open, not quite in public but certainly not in a secure environment.'

'Get up the road then,' said Clarissa. 'I'll see Lady Angela about this.'

'With all due respect,' said Patterson, 'let Sabine do it.'

'Why?'

'These women,' said Patterson, 'they're very—how shall I put this—they like to be their own boss. They're not used to taking orders. They're not used to people answering back in their face. Take this morning, for instance.'

'I was out last night, Pats, for goodness' sake,' said Clarissa.

'No, no, even beyond that, you're the boss. You're not seen as someone they can instruct. Send Sabine because she understands the arts and the items. She'll be able to tell you if those are real carriages that are there tonight or if at any time they've been switched. But she's also not the DI; she's not the one that they have to try to be superior over.'

'Good call, Pats,' said Clarissa. 'Make sure you smarten up, Sabine. If she's having a do, she's not going to want you to be a mess—no jeans and t-shirts and that stuff.'

Sabine nodded, almost with a sigh. 'We'll be up soon. Maybe you can phone ahead, Pats, and let them know.'

Patterson nodded. 'I've also got something else.'

'What?' said Clarissa, almost surprised.

'I haven't just been sitting over that computer doing nothing and keeping out.'

'What then?' said Clarissa.

'I've been talking to agencies around the world trying to track down the movements of Garrick. Everyone's having problems tracking him.'

'That's the type of guy he is,' said Clarissa.

'No,' said Patterson. 'Listen, everyone's having problems in the sense that for two months nobody has seen sight nor sound of him. Not one moment. Has he let himself be seen out somewhere? As opposed to the previous years, he's completely unseen. Previously, he's always seen in places. He's always seen to be somewhere. Therefore, they're not looking for where he's not.'

'What are you saying?' asked Clarissa.

'Garrick has gone to ground the last two months. Garrick goes to ground, his carriage is stolen, nobody can find Garrick. Is Garrick the guy behind this? Has Garrick pulled a fast one?' asked Patterson. 'Is that a possibility?'

'Somebody's coming after them,' said Emmett. 'Garrick's a possibility.'

'He's making sure it's not moved on. Maybe he's taking the items himself.'

'No, no,' said Clarissa. 'Garrick doesn't do things like this personally. He's a collector. That makes little sense.'

'Then why's Garrick suddenly gone to ground? Why's he not being seen at all?' said Patterson.

'I don't know,' said Clarissa, 'but we need to find out.'

Chapter 17

S abine set her compact case down inside the hotel room and collapsed onto the bed. She'd have to get back up on her feet shortly, but she was tired. Up to Inverness, down to Glasgow, run around, look for this person. Back out you come; up we go again. She had hoped Christmas would be quiet this year. There were plans that Emmett and she had to partake in one of his gaming sessions. Some sort of festive role-playing, involving somebody called the Krampus.

Oh, well, thought Sabine, *that one's on the back burner for next year.*

She needed to see Lady Angela, and sharpish. She'd phoned the woman, asking if she could attend the do but the woman had insisted on meeting her. And then saying that she could only meet her at approximately six o'clock. Sabine had rushed up to Inverness. Now she was throwing her bags into the hotel and would have to run out in the car soon.

Emmett had asked to come with her, but she told him no. He needed to get a rest, too. Emmett would look after the large carriage, at least prior to it reaching the parade. Clarissa didn't want to be hamstrung to one particular place.

Patterson was better served working his computer and

deciding where the rest of the family linked in—indeed, who was family. And so, Emmett had drawn the task of looking after the large carriage. It wasn't going into action until the next day, however, so he had time and a chance to put his feet up. Sabine would not deprive him of that.

Sabine, however, was struggling to see how this case was going to be solved before Christmas. Surely she wouldn't be expected to work Christmas Day? Although this was the twenty-third, the parade was tomorrow night, so more than likely Christmas Day would be spent up in this part of the world.

She wasn't doing anything back home. She had previously said to Emmett about maybe going out, booking a Christmas meal somewhere, or even just having something simple between the two of them. Emmett said that some of his friends invited him round. More games on Christmas Day might have been a good idea, but that was out the window.

She glanced up at the clock in the room. Sabine reckoned she'd better get going; otherwise, she'd miss her appointment with Lady Angela. Do that and getting into the evening soiree would be even harder. She had thought about changing, but she didn't have time. So, Sabine walked out to the car, still in her blue jeans, boots, and t-shirt.

Lady Angela's wasn't that far away, and as she pulled up to the rather glamorous monstrosity of a house, she could see plenty of people busily running around. A large Christmas tree had been erected outside the front door which she couldn't remember anybody mentioning before. As she went to ring the doorbell, the door was opened by a butler who said that Sabine was expected.

He almost glided through the different hallways until Sabine was taken into the drawing room. Lady Angela was standing, already dressed up for the evening. Earrings hung off her ears like chandeliers. A large voluminous blue dress meant when she turned to walk over to Sabine, it was almost like she ghosted across, her feet and legs lost somewhere underneath her.

'You must be Urquhart's woman.'

Sabine nearly spat out in laughter. Urquhart's woman? When had she ever been Urquhart's woman?

'I'm Detective Sergeant Sabine Ferguson and yes, my boss is Detective Inspector Urquhart,' she said. Pulling out a warrant card, she displayed towards the woman. 'I wanted to talk to you about the soiree you're having this evening, that you're taking the carriages to.'

'Yes, yes. Just a little show with some friends. Why? What's the issue?'

'I'd like to accompany them, or to be there.'

'Certainly not. It's a private thing, for the girls and me. We don't want riffraff.'

'I don't have to be with you. I need to be in the vicinity. Just for protection of the carriages. You understand? We've had three gone missing.'

'Yes, I'd heard another one had gone missing. Really, you guys need to get on top of this, and fast. I don't know what the public pay you for.'

There was almost an implication that maybe Angela didn't pay, which aggrieved Sabine slightly.

'So, it's okay if I accompany you?'

'No, it is not. I don't see the point. They're my friends. Nothing's going to happen to them.'

'Well, I think it's best if I'm there. If we lose these, there's only the one carriage left. Clearly, whoever is after them is out for the collection.'

'If you're insisting on coming along,' said Lady Angela, 'you're certainly not coming along like that.' She glared at Sabine's outfit.

'It's what I usually wear,' said Sabine.

'Not to one of these soirees, you don't. You'll have to be dressed up somewhat better. You look like one of those action-figure women. T-shirts these days—I mean, could they make them any tighter?'

Lady Angela certainly didn't have a figure that would have suited one of these T-shirts. Sabine took offence at how she was being targeted, but being a consummate professional, she simply said, 'I'll be dressed appropriately.'

'I expect a gown at least,' said Lady Angela.

'I won't be wearing a gown,' said Sabine. 'I will, however, be dressed in smart trousers and a jacket. I will be in the background.'

'A gown, I insist,' said Lady Angela. 'Either that or get out of here. At least that woman had some sort of style. Every time I've seen her on the television, she's dressed in Scottishness at least.'

'Again, I won't be wearing a gown,' said Sabine, 'because if someone tries to take the carriages, I need to run. I won't be here to enjoy myself but to perform a function, and that is the protection of the carriages.'

'If you insist,' said Lady Angela, 'but black and white.'

'That's fine. I've got a white blouse. If I could get to—'

'You can't get to see them. They've already been wrapped up and on the route.' And—'

There was a knock at the door. It opened, and the butler

came in. He bowed before Lady Angela. 'Apologies for interrupting you, Your Ladyship, but there's a phone call.'

'And who is it?'

'I believe it's Miss McNeice from Hamper Holdings.'

'Excellent.'

Lady Angela turned and marched over to a phone that was sitting on one of the tables. She picked it up and held it to her ear. 'Ah, Mater, yes, dreadful news, dreadful news. No, I'm still out this evening. I'm still letting the girls have a look. Of course we'll be taking care. You never could trust Katie with anything. You know that. Yes, yes. Our arrangement's going fine. Good, good. Yes, yes, they've been here too. I've got one of them here at the moment. Selena or something, you call this one.'

Sabine almost grimaced, but held her perfect countenance. 'Sabine' wasn't a tough name after all.

Sabine stayed waiting while Lady Angela continued her call, almost ignorant of Sabine standing there. Eventually, Lady Angela went to put the phone down. 'Goodbye, Mater. Yes, will see you soon. Love to all.'

The phone went down, and then Lady Angela walked over to Sabine. 'As I was saying, you'd better get dressed. Don't be late. We'll get the address to you. The soiree's kicking off around about eight o'clock. I don't want to see you before half past seven. Nothing worse than hanging around, standing around for hours beforehand, never mind during it.'

'Won't be a problem,' said Sabine. And she went to turn away when Lady Angela reached out and grabbed her shoulder.

'And that hair—brush it, woman. Ponytails are for little girls, not for a woman of your age.'

My age, thought Sabine. *I'm not that old.*

She ignored the rebuke, however, and left for the door, which was opened from the outside by the butler. The butler only gave her a smile as he led her towards the door. Sabine stopped him as she got there.

'Her Ladyship said that the carriages are already on their way?'

'That's correct, ma'am,' he said.

'How are they being transported?'

'There's a small van we have on this estate. They'll be going in the back of it. It's one of Her Ladyship's men. Well, a couple of them, actually. The larger carriage is hard to lift about.'

'And they've already been packed, have they?'

'I believe so. They've left, the men who are with them, and heading over now.'

'Very good. And what time will Her Ladyship be heading that way?'

'I don't think it's my business to discuss Her Ladyship's arrangements.'

'I am protecting Her Ladyship tonight as much as the carriages,' said Sabine. 'A brief detail on her movements would be most appreciated.'

'Well, if you put it that way, Her Ladyship will be arriving at eight o'clock on the dot, which means she'll leave here around about twenty to eight. It's not far.'

'Excellent,' said Sabine. 'I shall see her at her friend's.'

Sabine stepped out and felt the cold air hit her. She wrapped her jacket around her as she got into the car. Picking her phone up, she called Emmett.

'I'm coming back to get changed and go straight out. I haven't got a lot of time.'

'Have you eaten?' asked Emmett.

'Of course I haven't eaten.'

'Do you want me to get for you?'

'Like what?' said Sabine.

'I can walk to the chippy? Bring a Chinese back to the room here? You could pop in, have a quick bite before you go?'

'I'll be fine,' said Sabine.

'In that case, good luck,' said Emmett. He closed down the call.

Sabine sat back in the car as she drove along. Emmett was one of the best, she thought. There weren't many colleagues who looked out for you in the basics. Yes, if you'd been in a fight, if you'd been knocked down, of course, they'd come to your aid. But Emmett was looking out for your general welfare. She wasn't used to that. Clarissa wouldn't have gone and got her chips. Clarissa wouldn't have got you a coffee. No, maybe that was a little unfair.

As she continued to drive, she thought back to the conversation she'd heard on the phone. 'Mater,' she'd said. McNeice from Hamper Holdings. She'd called her 'Mater.' Twice! She activated the hands free on her phone and called Patterson.

'Eric,' she said. 'How are we getting on?'

'Still digging deep in.'

'Can you look for birth certificates? Lady Angela and Katie Grouse. I think their mother is Isabel McNeice. The woman from Hamper Holdings.'

'What makes you say that?'

'Well, she's just called Lady Angela, and she's called her 'Mater' on the phone.'

'Really? I'll get on to that. Wonder if she's got any more siblings.'

'I think it's worth looking into McNeice then, look for her

history.'

'I will do,' said Patterson. 'Will you be up to the office tonight?'

'No, I'm out on duty. I'm looking after the two carriages. I've got a pass out of Lady Angela though I have to look smart.'

'When do you not look smart?'

'You know, apparently, my jeans and my T-shirt make me look a bit like a tart. She didn't say so much. Felt like she was saying it, though.'

Patterson was laughing on the other end. 'Good luck, then. We'll be at the end of the phone if you need us. I don't think Clarissa's going anywhere tonight.'

'Why is that?'

'She's waiting for a call. She's very keen about this bracelet. Bit annoyed she couldn't look into it herself.'

'You probably don't realise how valuable an item it is. I'm sad I didn't get to see it. I'll have to pop down before it all disappears away somewhere. You should take a look.'

'I don't really see it myself,' said Patterson. 'It's just something old.'

'As Clarissa would say, you're not tactile. Good on a computer, but not tactile,' said Sabine. 'Right, I've got to get to the hotel and get out. I'll let you know if there're any developments. You can keep the boss informed there.'

'I doubt you'll get away without being phoned at some point shortly. She's not sure what to do while she's waiting for this call.'

'I'll tell her I'm on duty. I don't need interruptions.'

Sabine closed down the call and continued her drive. *Mater, eh? Families. If there's a family involved in this, it'll be a mess,* thought Sabine. *It's always a mess when families are involved.*

She wondered what sort of family it was.

Chapter 18

Perry was a little perturbed. Hope had accompanied him down to London to go looking for this bracelet. Not only was it close to Christmas, and the flights cost an arm and a leg, but Hope was now pregnant. Perry had never been around a woman who was pregnant while working. He thought maybe she needed to take a step back. That she would be in the office was fine to him, but he was finding himself very protective of her.

'Perry, would you just walk?' said Hope. 'I don't need the help. I'm fine. I'm not heavily pregnant. And I'm good. Look at me, I'm glowing!'

She was glowing. Perry was not someone who was attracted to Hope, but he was a man, and yes, he understood how some were taken in by her height, her luscious red hair, and her fierce determination. At the moment, however, she was glowing even more so. Her hair, which was vibrant enough, seemed to be oozing a life. Perry wondered if he could get pregnant, if only to sort out his rather poor mop.

'Just take it easy. I'm sure you're tired. I'm sure you're . . .'

'You're sure of nothing, Perry. I am how I am, and at the moment I'm fine, and we've got a case to get on with. Despite you being out in the Cairngorms, it was right to call me in. We've got a dead man and we need to find out who he is. Besides, this isn't a run around. This is just asking questions, following a trail. We'll be fine.'

Perry wasn't so sure and still opened the door for Hope as he entered the offices of one professor in the London School of Economics.

'Hello,' said Hope. 'I'm Detective Inspector Hope McGrath. This is DC Perry Warren. DI Clarissa Urquhart sent us.'

Hope McGrath pulled up a picture on her phone and handed it to the old man who was sitting behind the desk in the room. He had grey hair, a rather dapper suit on, and smiled behind his small round brass glasses.

'Ooh,' he said suddenly. 'Now that's interesting.'

'Why is it interesting?'

'I keep an eye on these sorts of things. Call it a hobby, a habit, whatever. This was on the move not that long ago.'

'I'm sure of it. Can you tell me where and when?' said Hope.

'No, I can't tell you any of that detail. What I can do is put you in touch with a man who might. However, he's a rather unsavoury character. But he might be persuaded to help you.'

'How?'

'He doesn't like the law, he doesn't like anyone. He especially doesn't like DI Urquhart as he's had a run in with her in the past. Kind of owes her one, so I would call in that favour, but you might have to find him.'

'What's his name?' asked Perry.

'He's called Cyclops because he hasn't got two eyes, just the one—usually wears a patch over the other one. You can see him most times in this pub.' The man wrote down the address of a pub. 'You'll have to be quick, though. I guess you've got the advantage—he won't know you.'

'Really,' said Perry. 'Any other ways we can get a hold of him?'

The man was looking at Hope, rather unhealthily, Perry thought.

'He's one for the ladies. I think someone with your obvious attraction might haul him in, especially the scar. He'll like the scar. He'll think you're a bit of a rough one.'

'I am a bit of a rough one,' said Hope. 'He'd better believe it.'

Perry gave her a look, but Hope grabbed the piece of paper and thanked the professor. As they exited the room, Perry followed in short order.

'You're not serious. You're not seriously going to put yourself out as bait for him?'

'And why not? It's just a guy; it'll be easy. You'll be about, anyway. He will not assume you're with me.'

Perry went to say something, but then simply nodded. 'Of course he wouldn't. We could fly Susan down, let her do it rather than—'

'No,' said Hope. 'We're here now. Let's get out to this pub, wherever it is, see if we can bring the guy in.'

Sometimes there was no use debating with Hope. Especially when she made her mind up—she wasn't nasty about it, but she could be firm—so Perry simply put his head down and followed her.

They got a taxi out to the pub, and while standing outside, Hope said to Perry, 'If things do get rough, I'll get out. Don't become a hero, okay? You're not a fighter. I don't want you getting a bottle in the face or something. Don't worry about me. I can handle myself.'

'I know,' said Perry, 'but—'

'Perry, I'm pregnant, okay? I choose to come to work. If I'm not happy about that, I'll not come. Treat me as I should be treated, like I am just me.'

Perry wasn't sure. He guessed he was probably old school in that sense—woman with a child on board—you took care of them; you gave them every comfort, every help. Nowadays, it wasn't always the case; you saw pregnant ladies getting on the trains, nobody getting up for them. Nobody stood up in the buses to give them a seat.

Often it was older people that did it. The common courtesy, the belief that certain people are in a frailer state than you because of whatever reason, no longer applied. That was your seat, your choice. You got it first. You don't get up for anybody else. Some things had died that shouldn't have died.

Hope walked into the bar, and Perry followed. She went up to the counter and ordered herself an orange juice, while Perry went to the end of the bar and quietly ordered a non-alcoholic beer. It would be a dead giveaway if he was sitting there with an orange juice. A woman, not so.

As he looked up when his pint arrived, he saw Hope indicating for him to look to the corner. There was a man there with an eyepatch. He wore a dull grey t-shirt with a leather jacket and what looked like combat fatigues underneath.

Hope remained at the bar. It wasn't long before Perry saw the man make a move. He watched as the man swanned up close to Hope. He bought her a drink—another orange juice. But Perry watched his hand. Occasionally, it came across and touched hers. Then his hand was on her knee. She was doing well, though. She was feigning interest.

And then she was leaning in towards him. What did she say to him? 'We need to go somewhere quieter?'

Hope was up on her feet, walking ahead of the man, a hand casually left behind, which he took and went with her. Perry was up like a shot, exited the door approximately five seconds after they did and saw her walking down the street with him. They were hand in hand now, and she cut down an alleyway.

Perry ran but slowed down sufficiently distant from it so he wouldn't run in like a huffing and puffing clown. Slowly, he peered round the corner, expecting to see Hope in a difficult position to come to her rescue. Instead, she was standing there, holding the man up against the wall, pushing hard on his chest.

'Ah, there you are, Perry. Our friend Cyclops here was just going to talk to us about the bracelet.'

'Good,' said Perry, a bit lost for words, but Hope gave him a smile.

'What happened with the bracelet?'

'It was a find,' said Cyclops, 'dug out of the ground and then it got lifted. One of the gangs from the east end had lifted it. No idea what they got. I think it moved on as part of a large group of items across the dealer, Mr Brinks. Brinks was clever though, sold it on and then eventually word of it got out and around. Some heavy hitter wanted it. Lando from here, he had it. Well, when he was alive.'

'The thing is, it's quite a small bracelet. If you put it on your wrist, you're not likely to get it back off again.'

'Lando put it on his wrist, did he?' said Perry.

'Said nobody would take it off him. Said nobody was going to nick it off him. They found him with his wrist chopped.'

'Oh,' said Hope. 'Lovely.'

'His hand was lying there, the rest of him beside it, bracelet gone.'

'Do you know who did it?' asked Hope.

'Good idea. Don't know who wanted it, though. Nobody knows who wanted it. And when that happened, nobody asked questions. Something like that isn't worth having if all it ends up is giving you a stump for a hand, or even a grave.'

'Who did it?' asked Hope.

'You might find him hanging out around, well, the Crosbys. Check for the Crosby gang. Mathieu. Mathieu Crosby. He's the one you're looking for. Better be careful. He's not like me. I'm a ladies' man. I like my face, and I like ladies to like me so I don't treat them bad.'

'You don't, do you?' said Hope. 'I hope not. Otherwise, I might have to come find you.'

'Not that bad. Not unless they like it that way.' Hope pressed hard on his chest. The man wheezed.

'You still don't treat them that way, even if they do like it,' she said. She turned to Perry. 'Do we know the Crosbys?'

'We know people who might.'

'We best get on then,' said Hope. 'You, however, you be a good boy; otherwise, I'll come back.'

'You can come back any time you want, darling,' said the man.

Perry could have hit him, but Hope just laughed in his face. She turned and walked with Perry to the end of the alleyway, back out onto the street.

'We need to visit the locals,' she said. 'They'll know who the Crosbys are. I hope they know how to get them.'

They walked along before hailing down a cab and climbed inside. As they drove along, there was silence between the pair of them until Hope broke it. 'What?' she said.

'Sorry if you think I'm overstepping the mark,' said Perry, 'but you know you need to understand that this baby—well, we're all excited, you know. I know Ross has got a kid, but this is a baby. The team's not had a baby before.'

'Neither have I, and you have no idea how precious it is to me, Perry. So trust me when I say I'll look after it.'

He nodded and looked out the window. There was silence until Hope spoke.

'So, this bracelet that moved on and was wanted by someone. So our man up in the north, he must be a nasty piece of work too, if he's gone to this trouble to get it. He's actually sent someone to cut the hand off to bring the bracelet back. We're not dealing with anybody nice.'

'We're on the murder squad, Hope. When do we deal with nice people?'

'But you know what I mean. He's the victim here, and yet it looks like he might not have been. Looks like he might have sent a lot of other people up. It's brutal to come and cut the hand off someone just because he couldn't get the bracelet off.'

'Indeed. We best watch our backs,' said Perry.

The local police station was not far off, just a short taxi ride away, and Hope introduced herself at the front desk. She was taken up with Perry to where the detective offices were all arranged on a single floor. She was introduced to DI Lorraine Busby.

Hope related the story while Busby sat there. She was an older woman than Hope, possibly in her fifties, elegantly tall but with a worn face. As Hope told her story, her piercing eyes watched Hope closely with a glance over towards Perry, occasionally.

'You can certainly pick them. Mattieu Crosby. We're going after the Crosbys tonight, performing a raid on them. Mattieu could be there. I don't mind you tagging along as long as you don't get in the way. By all means, pull him to one side.'

'Thank you. That sounds good.'

'However,' said Lorraine, 'if I need to call this off, you'll have to stay away from him. I can't risk them thinking we're on to them. We're on a go tonight, but if for any reason it doesn't happen, I'd like you to stay away from him.'

Hope nodded. She wasn't sure she would, but she would not have an argument now in case it didn't need to happen.

Lorraine Busby looked at her watch. 'You've maybe got about four hours. I suggest you get yourself something to eat—some delightful spots around here. Meet me back here in another two hours. You can join in the last of the briefing and then we get off and get done.'

Hope stood up to shake the woman's hand. 'Gives us a chance anyway,' said Hope. 'Thank you for that.'

She walked out with Perry, whose eyes were once again casting an aspersion that Hope was maybe pushing things too far.

'We're just following. We're tagging along and then we'll ask him questions. I'm not rushing in. I'm not daft, Perry.'

'Never said you were.'

'Your eyes did. Can I tell you something?'

'What?' said Perry.

'Susan. Susan Cunningham. You liked her, didn't you?'

'Very much.'

'You were kind to her. You were unbelievably kind to her. But Susan's an independent woman, Perry. You need to understand those of us who are like that. We don't want someone coming to our every need. We want somebody with us, alongside us. You tried too hard with Susan. I think she might have been there; she might have even got past that age barrier. You tried too hard. Sorry.'

'What?'

She walked ahead of him for a few steps before turning to see a moping Perry.

'Oh cheer up. Most men of your age don't even get a girl like that interested in you. You did better than most. Come on, let's go find a curry.'

Chapter 19

Sabine stood in a rather grandiose hall at the evening soiree that Lady Angela was attending. Towards the front of the hall were two tiny podiums, prepared for the carriages. The carriages had arrived outside the building, attended to by some of Lady Angela's people. Meanwhile, inside, the guests were mingling, and Sabine thought she was very out of place.

She was dressed in a smart black suit with a white blouse underneath, something that crossed the lines between casual and smart. It worked for her in many places, for she could never be sure just how to pitch things. This suit hit the middle ground, allowing her to blend in, or even act as a waitress if she wanted to. It was that sort of non-formal yet formal outfit.

What may have given her away were the shoes she was wearing. There was no high heel, and if anything, they were closer to a hiking boot than they were to a fashionable shoe. They did, however, afford the luxury of being able to run hard if she needed to.

Sabine's other problem in trying not to stand out was that she was tall, with long black hair, which Lady Angela insisted didn't go into a ponytail. As such, Sabine had brushed her hair out several times, and let it sit on her shoulders, making people think she actually might be a guest. Of course, on arrival Lady Angela told her in no way was she to fraternise with her friends; rather, Sabine should stay in the background.

Which, of course, was all Sabine ever wanted. Sabine had also spoken to those who had delivered the carriages and had seen both carriages in the back of a van. There was a small team of three men, two of whom were rather elderly with the third being a young lad. The carriages were stored securely in the van, a protective covering over them.

The plan was for them to be paraded in—the lights should be dimmed a little—music blaring, and Lady Angela and her friends would watch. It would take two men to bring in one of the carriages. The first one could be carried by one, but Sabine thought they might use two, anyway. The carriages would come in one by one as well, something Lady Angela had insisted on; otherwise, they would look like a job lot.

Sabine wondered how you could ever talk about these items as being a job lot, but then again, Lady Angela didn't seem to be one who appreciated them for their magic.

A waiter approached Sabine, offering her a glass of champagne on a tray, and Sabine shook her head. She looked around the room. Everyone was certainly upper class, at the higher end of society. Not that Sabine had anything against them, it was just that she wasn't used to being in this crowd. Lately she'd been going out with Emmett to his gaming evenings, and the people there were anything but upper class. Erudite, yes, but not upper class.

She strolled round the room, looking at various other items that were on display. There was much jewellery on display. When she got close, she could see that the value was nothing compared to the carriages.

Lady Angela, dressed immaculately, swept over to Sabine, her large dress gown almost billowing as she approached.

'I take it everything is to your satisfaction, Detective Sergeant?'

'It looks okay. Your men are stationed with the items.'

'We'll be bringing them in presently. I must say, it's a fantastic evening. Good turnout. I'm sure the charities will do well out of it.'

'It's a charity event?' said Sabine, feeling she had to make conversation.

'Of course. When you have been given so much in life as I have, I feel you have to give back.'

'Well, that's decent of you,' said Sabine.

She looked over Lady Angela's shoulder at the many guests parading in outfits that could probably buy a family dinner for the year. Lady Angela, clearly not impressed with the conversation she was having, strode off. Sabine wondered if any of them ever did time in a soup kitchen, got down onto the streets, or got their hands dirty. Maybe she was being hard. Maybe some of them did. This just didn't seem like helping people particularly. It seemed more like a big shindig.

A few minutes later, Sabine was stationed by the door of the room and two footmen opened the doors before the lights were suddenly dimmed, and music played. There was almost a glitter ball effect from certain lights at the front of the hall. Suddenly, on a small platform carried by two of Lady Angela's men, appeared one carriage.

It was the smaller one. Obviously, the idea of the bigger one would be even more impressive—but not necessarily the case, thought Sabine. She watched as they went past. She looked carefully, and then she froze for a moment. It was hard to tell in the light. She'd never seen one, of course, until the other day, but you knew what they should be, you knew what they should look like, you knew of the quality. She stared as the item was carried forward up to the podium and placed on it.

She was going to stride forward, but suddenly there was an almost swooping of Lady Angela's contingent as the carriage was placed on the podium. To get through that melee would be difficult. The two porters, however, left the room before she could get out. Then the music started again, and they came back in with the second one. The men were struggling with this one, a little heavier. But again, Sabine looked at it and wondered. Was that definitely it? Or was the light playing tricks on her? It was awkward because there were strobes going off and the men almost moved in staccato.

Carefully, Sabine glided around the outside of the room up towards the first podium where the smaller carriage had been placed. The numbers of people thronged suddenly over to the second one, allowing Sabine to get closer. She stared along the wheels, looked into the interior. She stared up inside the roof of the carriage and then round to the back. Her heart thumped.

Lady Angela, by this time, had migrated back in between both carriages. Most of the contingent had fallen back to a polite distance, as it was obvious she was going to speak. Sabine, however, was still looking at the first carriage. She then turned to walk over to the second one, moving right behind Lady Angela, who gave a cough as she was ready to speak.

Sabine ignored her, looking at the wheels of the larger carriage, then looking at the interior. *That isn't right,'* thought

Sabine. She reached over and touched the front end of the carriage, looking at a gold rim. *That doesn't look right. The join is . . . that's been put together and looks to be covered up. That's not a single piece flowing through. It should be a single piece.* She continued to move round the carriage and then heard a voice.

'Excuse me, do you mind? If you'd kindly step back and let me begin.'

She looked over at Lady Angela, who was staring at her with daggers.

'I think we may have a problem,' said Sabine.

'I do have a problem. You! Get out of the way. I'm ready to speak.'

She looked like one of those comic-opera singers. The waist tucked in, with an impossible chest above and a voice that looked ready to shake the gods from their slumber. But Sabine was unmoved.

'We've got a problem,' she said, quieter than how she'd been spoken to. Sabine turned and fled from the room, running out through the double doors. She could hear the shock behind her, but she didn't stop, instead running out to where the vans were. The two men who had carried the carriages inside were still in the room, but that left the young lad outside.

As Sabine got there, she saw the van that had brought the carriages. She looked in the front, but there was no one there. Running round to the back, she pulled at the door, and it came away freely, unlocked.

Looking inside the van, she saw a figure at the far end. She jumped up, ran over, and put her hand down to the figure's head. She tilted it up towards her. That was the young lad. He was out cold. She reached down and touched his neck. Yes, he was out cold, but there was a pulse there. She exited the van, jumping out to see the hordes of party goers coming out through the front door. They spied her, and Lady Angela at the front roaring towards her.

'What? What's going on? What's the meaning of this?'

'Need the gateman. I need the guy at the gate,' said Sabine.

The location of the party was a rather posh house indeed, with a large hall, but the gate had been manned that evening. Sabine ran the length of the driveway, which wound down through trees until it reached the front road.

As she approached, a man dressed in a smart uniform smiled at her. 'Oh, good evening again, Detective Sergeant,' he said. 'Everything all right?'

'No, it's not,' said Sabine. 'Who's gone out of here recently?'

'Just one of the catering vans. They were late with one of the cakes.'

'Did you search it?' asked Sabine.

'I looked at it on the way in. There were some boxes there. Had "cake" on them.'

'Did you search it on the way out?'

'No, why would I? They had delivered the cake by then.'

'Registration,' said Sabine.

'Blimey, what's up?' said the man. His face was showing signs of worry.

'I think we've just had the principal items of the evening stolen,' said Sabine. She picked up her mobile phone and called into the station. 'Describe the van to me,' she said. 'Describe the van.'

'Quite simple. One of those hire vans, you know. Seven and a half tonner, at best. Probably smaller,' the man said. Sabine relayed the information to the desk sergeant, asking that all units that were out and about be advised to be on the lookout for a white seven and a half tonne van. She gave the company it had been hired from, words that were emblazoned along the side of the van.

She then phoned Clarissa, asking her to come down to the party. *Am I sure?* thought Sabine. *Those were definitely fakes, weren't they?* She found herself second-guessing. But no, she was right, and the van had gone.

She made her way back up to the hall, and was intercepted by one of the footmen. He said, 'Lady Angela would like to see you.'

Sabine was on the phone again as she walked back, calling an ambulance. The young lad lying in the van needed attended to. She wondered if anybody else had bothered.

'You can run back and tell Lady Angela I'm on my way up. The inspector's coming out as well. I believe she's had her items stolen.'

Sabine waved the man away as she walked back up. The guests had now returned back inside the hall, the cold outside being too much for them. It was as she reached the hallway that she received another phone call. This time, it was the desk sergeant.

'Sabine,' he said, 'I'm sorry to inform you, but we've got a van matching that description on fire.'

'Where?' she asked. The man gave the location and Sabine realised it was close to where she now stood. *Damn it,* she thought. *Right under my nose. Right here.*

She took a deep breath. Whoever it was had got five of them now; there was only the big one to go. It took about another twenty minutes for an ambulance to arrive, by which time the young lad who had escorted the carriages had come to.

In the presence of the paramedics, Sabine questioned him.

He was woozy, but all he would say was, 'The young man or woman.' Sabine, brushing off Lady Angela, got hold of the porters who had carried the items in.

'He was sitting in the van the whole time,' they said. 'The other van had pulled up. We saw it. But he was in the front of the van, the young lad. Jim was in there.'

'Are you sure it was him?'

'Yes,' they said.

'You see,' said Sabine, 'Jim says that you two went in first time, to check things were ready. That's when he was attacked and then put into the back of the van. Whoever you saw in the front must have been the attacker.'

'Well, it looked like a boy to me. I mean, it was Jim. Had Jim's hat on and that.'

Clarissa will be here soon, and she wouldn't be happy, thought Sabine. But it struck Sabine—*it was the flasher, the peeping tom, not particularly masculine. Was this figure a man? Was it a boy? How could they see a boy there? It would take somebody with a bit of strength, or somebody with an accomplice. You could be in the back of the van while she—or he—sat in the front pretending to be the lad. They'd been played, certainly, and played well.*

Even though she didn't think the security was up to much, she took a seat, gathering herself, for tonight was going to be a long one. Lady Angela would demand answers, and Clarissa would tear the place up for them.

Chapter 20

Hope, standing at the back, watched as the meeting closed, observing the many people preparing to do their job tonight. Her mind was focused on Mattieu Crosby, and while she hoped that the rest of the operation went well, he was the one she needed to get. He was the one who would know about the bracelet. Cyclops had put Hope down this path by giving them the name of Mattieu Crosby.

And now the local enforcement agencies were already preparing to swoop on him as part of the Crosby gang. Hope had watched them explain how they were going to infiltrate and circle a building, and then capture the entire gang unawares. Detective Inspector Lorraine Busby had been happy enough for Hope to come along. However, she'd asked that they remain well back when the operation was taking place.

It was fair enough, Hope reckoned. After all, the woman was running the show, and if it was the opposite way around, Hope wouldn't like somebody from half the nation away to come and interrupt her. And it was their patch. They knew what they were doing here. They knew the streets.

Instead, Perry and Hope would wait in the police car until

they'd apprehended Mattieu Crosby. It was courtesy, really. There was no need for them even to be there. They could wait in the station until he was brought back.

But Hope was an officer, and officers wouldn't do that to each other—push you that far away. Besides, you never knew when you might need an extra body.

As they made their way down to the cars to begin the operation, Perry and Hope were told to go to a car driven by a young constable. He was in plain clothes at this time, and Hope sat in the front seat beside him with Perry in the back. They waited while the other cars drove out before they hit the streets in a rather drab brown hatchback.

'What's your name?' asked Hope.

'Constable Alexander,' he said. 'Alex Alexander.'

'Your parents just have no imagination,' said Perry. It was almost as if he said it before realising he had done. But the young man smiled.

'Something like that.'

'I'm Detective Inspector Hope McGrath. Hope for tonight, Alex. This is DC Perry Warren. Perry for the night.'

'Pleased to meet you. I wasn't expecting to get out on this. They sort of called me in. I think I'm . . . well, I shouldn't say it, should I?'

'You're babysitting,' said Hope. 'We don't know where we're going. We don't know the area. It's fine. The DI's been good at letting us out here. Don't worry. We will not make your life awkward.'

The young man smiled, but Hope could see the nervousness in his hands as he gripped the wheel. Maybe this was his first time out in a proper raid. It wouldn't be hers, and it wouldn't be Perry's. Hope sat back to enjoy the show, knowing that she was there to do very little.

The building they were raiding was near the Docklands area of London, right down on the river. As they approached, Constable Alexander pulled the car up to one side.

'We'll not go any closer. The rest of them will move in. Are you okay with that? You don't want to see more?'

'If this is where Inspector Busby told you to wait, then here we'll wait,' said Hope. 'She's the boss tonight.'

'Yes,' said Alexander. Yet again, he was gripping the wheel, his hands almost sweaty.

'Take it easy,' said Hope. 'We're just going to sit here. There's not a lot going to happen.'

'Some people there might be armed,' said the constable. 'I've not really gone in against armed people before. I'm not long off the beat.'

'Well, all good learning for you,' said Hope.

She sat in silence, only hearing the occasional fidgeting of Perry behind her. She imagined in the old days he would sit there with a cigarette in his mouth, the car filling up with clouds of smoke. But not today. These days, he just fidgeted.

Hope turned on the police radio, selected the band they needed, and heard Inspector Busby giving instructions. So far, it seemed to be pretty textbook; they were closing in. They had caught sight of key people they wanted to grab, including Mattieu.

'You know anything about Mattieu Crosby?' asked Hope.

'Nasty piece of work,' said the constable. 'Very nasty piece of work. Can handle himself.'

'Well, let's just hope they bring him in nice and easy then,' said Hope.

She sat back, listening to the radio. Bit by bit, the capture squad snuck in, infiltrating into the compound the warehouse was inside of, and then they reached the warehouse itself. They grabbed a couple of people on the way, and now the pace was quickening.

Hope heard the go-call on the comms, as everyone raced in. They were calling out who they had, who they'd grabbed. She heard gunfire, and then it was quiet. The names of who they were capturing were being relayed through. Hope was listening intently, listening for Mattieu.

As she sat in the car, she realised that the constable in the driver's seat was suddenly leaning forward.

'Something up?' asked Hope, thinking she'd missed something on the communications.

'There,' he said. 'Walking up the street. Mattieu Crosby!'

'That man?' said Hope. There was a man, approximately six feet four tall, and built like a warrior from a fantasy film. He had clearly evident muscles, courtesy of a sleeveless T-shirt. The man looked agitated, almost trying to get out of the way. He wore jeans and what looked like strong, solid boots. There was a scar running across one of his cheeks—not that Hope put any negativity on scars these days, having obtained her own.

'Are you sure it's him?' asked Hope.

'That's him. That's him,' said the agitated constable.

Hope picked up the radio and called in to the detective inspector. 'Constable Alexander has identified Mattieu Crosby. He's passing our position at the moment.'

'He's where?' came the call. 'How did he get through the net?'

'Do you want me to apprehend?' said Hope.

'If you don't, we won't get him. Tell Constable Alexander to apprehend him.'

Beside her, the young constable looked with fear in his eyes, but he swallowed hard and started getting out of the car.

Perry leaned in from the rear of the car. 'That guy there,' he said. 'She wants that kid to stop that guy there?'

'That's what she said,' said Hope.

'I'd better give him a hand then,' said Perry. 'The man looks like he can handle himself.'

'He does, doesn't he? I'm coming with you,' said Hope.

'No, you're not. You're not getting involved in fisticuffs like this. No need to.'

'Perry, I outrank you. Now shut up. Let's go.'

Hope stepped out of the car, and only for a moment did she think that this was the first time she was taking two people into a fight. She put it to the back of her mind, however.

Constable Alexander was out in front of the car, walking ahead of Hope. She watched the man close in on the other figure. He announced who he was, told the man he was under arrest and to stop. The man pulled a knife.

Alexander went to move towards him, but the man was quick, struck accurately, and the knife pierced Alexander's shoulder. From where Hope was, she believed that was where the man intended to strike, not towards the heart or the neck. Quite possibly, the fact he was a police officer saved Alexander. He did, however, hit the ground like a ton of bricks, clutching his shoulder, shouting.

'Perry, flank him,' said Hope.

'I can take him,' said Perry.

No, you can't, thought Hope, but she wasn't going to announce that in front of their suspect. They closed to within about ten feet of the man, who didn't look like he was going to run. Perry was flanking him down the side, but the man was coming towards Hope.

'You want a bit of this too, do you? I've already got one bit of blood on it. I might not go for your shoulder; might even take you with me.'

It was unusual for Hope to stare up at her suspect, but the man had four inches on her, and he was certainly bigger. Hope kept closing on him, hoping to bait him forward to attack her, and allow Perry time to get round the back.

Perry was not a good fighter. He would have been more like Clarissa—he would fight dirty. But the primary worry for Hope was the knife the man had. If she had a taser gun, she could have hit him with it.

She didn't carry weapons, normally. She wasn't about to start tonight on somebody else's operation. They would have had to ask her in on that one. Being out in a remote car and standing well clear, she didn't even have a stab vest on, unlike Constable Alexander. That being said, it hadn't done him much good when the knife had gone into his shoulder.

'Come on then,' said Hope. 'Let's have you.'

'Bloody Scotchie too,' said the man. He swung the knife in front and Hope leaned back, the blade whizzing in front of her. She then reached inside as his hand came back, grabbing the man's wrist, her other hand going up to grab his other one. Suddenly, the pair of them were in a clinch.

She could feel the man's force though, and was fighting hard to keep his hands from closing. What she had done was stall him for a moment, and that was all Perry needed.

Hope had never seen Perry as someone with alacrity, but like some sort of enormous sack of potatoes, he ran at the man from behind. Taking to the air, Perry leapt on his back, his arms swinging round the man's neck. *He'd have done better to kick him hard behind the knees,* thought Hope, *take him to the ground.* Maybe Perry was hoping his weight would do that. Instead, Perry simply clung to him like a limpet.

The man still struggled, and his left hand became free, reaching back to grab Perry's hair. Perry shouted, but only for a moment, and Hope could see him biting the man. Hope, however, was still worried about the knife and she took her now free hand up to join her first one and twisted the man's arm violently at the wrist. The knife clattered to the ground and Hope kicked it away.

She drove an elbow up into the man's throat. He started to choke, his hand slipping off Perry's hair. Perry was bouncing on him, trying to drive him to the ground. Hope kicked out at his knees and the man tumbled. He fell hard to the ground, Perry on top of him. But Perry didn't move, pinning him.

Hope took her handcuffs from out of her rear pocket, slapped one on a wrist. She drove her knee into the man's back, grabbing the other wrist that was flailing. With Perry's help, she brought the two wrists together and was able to put the handcuffs on Mattieu. She then got Perry to kneel with a knee across the man's back so he couldn't get up, while they waited for backup to come.

'Who the hell are you, anyway? I haven't seen you about here,' shouted Mattieu.

Hope replaced Perry on the man's back, allowing Perry to call for an ambulance. Alexander was still bloody and although talking, was in a deep state of shock. Hope could understand that.

As she placed a knee into the back of Mattieu, she took out her phone with a photograph of the bracelet. She wanted answers soon, and if she waited until he was brought in, processed, and then got into an interview room, she'd be the last to speak to him. This was her chance to get things moving before the processes kicked in. She put her phone down in front of his face.

'See that bracelet? Where did that bracelet go?'

The man looked up at her. 'What the hell? About the bracelet? Is this all about the bracelet?'

'Where did that bracelet go?' repeated Hope.

'Not worth hardly anything, that. All this, all this, just to get me.'

'That's a bronze-aged bracelet. It's practically priceless,' said Hope. 'Where did it go?'

'Bastard,' said the man, spitting. 'The bastard. He told me it was nothing. He told me—'

'He got you to hang on to it, because you're a tough nut. You wouldn't take any nonsense, and people wouldn't think you would peddle it,' said Hope. 'You were duped. Who did you give it to?'

'The bastard. Bloody Garrick. I said we shouldn't deal with him. I said it. Pa said we should deal with him. Bastard.'

The man spat out more expletives. But Hope picked her phone back up, scrolled through until she got an image of the dead man from the Cairngorms. She put the phone back in front of Mattieu.

'Still, at least the bugger's dead now,' grinned Mattieu, looking at the new image.

Chapter 21

Emmett was feeling tired. He'd popped along to help Sabine and Clarissa at the soiree where the two carriages had been stolen. It was difficult to come up with anything. Forensics would have to deal with the burnt-out van to see if they could get any DNA from it. But Emmett was interested to note that the potential thief seemed to have this androgynous feel about them. It had been a theme through too many encounters, and it meant something. Emmett was sure of it.

After he turned up at the house where the soiree had taken place, he carried out some investigations with Clarissa. Then Emmett had been sent off to the next carriage. Sabine was the officer who had been there, so Clarissa wanted her to finish off the details around the soiree. Clarissa was the overall boss, and Patterson was still working hard, rounding everything up, so Emmett was sent off to see to the last carriage.

It had been the middle of the night working with Clarissa, but when he arrived at Hamper Holdings, it was almost five in the morning. The staff had gone, at least the bulk of those who were doing the packing. Everything had been finished a few hours early, according to one of the foreman.

Now, it was just the last-minute delivery department. Special orders being sent out, dropped at doors, for this was Christmas Eve, and all the hampers would be there by lunchtime. That being said, Emmett found that Davi was still there.

The man looked as he had been described to Emmett: mad white hair, podgy belly with the jacket, and the trousers that looked like they hadn't been ironed in a month of Sundays. He was, however, quite amiable as Emmett approached him.

'Detective Sergeant Emmett Grump. I'm here to keep an eye on you and the carriage before it moves off.'

'It goes off later today,' said Davi. 'In fact, my girl's just arrived.'

'Your girl?' queried Emmett.

'She's going to be taking it in the van. The van's just come in,' said Davi. 'Come!'

He led Emmett through the building, out into the rear yard, where all the trucks were lined up, ready to take the hampers out. There was another truck off to one side. It was white, with a simple tailgate at the back.

'It'll elongate that tailgate. We'll have to lift it,' said Davi, 'and then we roll it in. She was here earlier on, about three, but she had to go again. Tailgate wasn't the right size.'

'Didn't she know what she was putting in it?' asked Emmett.

'She thought it would fit, but it didn't. It doesn't matter,' said Davi, 'because she's come back. We gave the carriage a trial run at getting into the van but it didn't fit. We had to do it on our own too, as the packers were still busy. But we realised it was too big, and she went off for another van.'

'Where is she?' asked Emmett. 'I'd just like to put a face to who's doing it, in case there are any issues in Inverness. I'll know who to look for.'

'Okay. Come,' said Davi. The man shuffled along in front of Emmett, almost tottering but something about him just didn't work for Emmett. He went up a flight of stairs and found the staff canteen. It was quiet at the moment, one woman manning the kitchen.

'Everyone's gone home,' said Davi. 'Worked through parts of the night, so doesn't need to be anybody here. We can have some breakfast if you want.'

Emmett took him up on his offer, and Davi and Emmett then took the loaded trays across to find a young woman sitting down at a table on her own. She wore a cap with black hair coming out of the rear in a tied-up ponytail. Despite this, the hair looked as if it would be voluminous, certainly not straight. She had a petite frame, too, and Emmett wondered about her as a truck driver. Maybe he was being funny, though. She wore a black anorak with black jeans beneath it, and as Emmett sat down, she gave a faint smile.

'This is Rash.'

'Rash?' said Emmett. 'That's an unusual name.'

'Just my nickname,' said the girl. 'It's what he calls me.'

'You've done things together before, then?'

'Rash is a friend. We've seen each other about before.'

'He knew me when I was younger,' said the girl. 'He knew my mother as well. Unfortunately, she's passed on now.'

'I'm sorry to hear that,' said Emmett.

'She was a lovely woman,' said Davi. 'Lovely woman. Gorgeous. Sad, she's gone. I look back and see it as a bad time.'

Emmett felt quite jolted by Davi. The man clearly wasn't the full shilling. And yet, part of Emmett didn't see it as a medical thing. He was a bit bemusing. Despite this, Emmett tucked into his scrambled egg, beans, and sausages, as did Davi. Rash, however, refused all offers of a drink.

'So tell me,' said Emmett, 'what's the plan for the carriage?'

'Truck's here,' said Rash, 'so I'll pick it up sometime after lunch. Take it down.'

'So what's happening with it at the moment?'

'It's locked up downstairs,' said Davi. 'I can show you. It's all locked up. Security, you know, we've got to have security. Truck's inside.'

'Do you mind if I see the truck before we go,' said Emmett, 'and also the carriage?'

'Of course,' said Rash. 'What's the problem?'

'I'm afraid several of these have been taken. You might not know, but the carriage is one of six, and five of them have disappeared, two last night. You may want somebody to accompany you when you take the items down.'

'I'll be okay,' said Rash. 'I have to do some last-minute Christmas shopping before then.'

'And I'm off to lunch,' said Davi. 'I'm going to eat with the staff. We do this, have a big Christmas lunch. And normally it's not a problem because we're not out at night. But the staff are coming to see the carriage. But they're not part of it. They're not working. There's just Rash, after she's done some last-minute Christmas shopping. She's going to take it down, and I'll be there too to see it and make sure it's okay. I'll hitch it up to the horses when it goes down to the fire station.'

'Very good,' said Emmett. 'And at the fire station, I believe there's plenty of people around, to keep an eye on it.'

'I won't leave the carriage either,' said Davi. 'It's a beautiful item.'

They finished their breakfast and Davi, shuffling along, led

Emmett down to the carriage with Rash following behind. Occasionally, Emmett turned and stared at her. She had a petite frame and something about her was reminding him of something, but he couldn't quite place it. She was very like a teenager, not engaging him much in conversation, and he reckoned she couldn't be that old.

Davi took them into the area for the carriage, punching in some codes before opening up the room. When he stepped inside, Emmett was impressed. The carriage did indeed look wonderful. Part of him wished Sabine had been here because she would have loved to have seen it, and she could do with a pickup. Clarissa was fuming at the moment, but it wasn't Sabine's fault. There should have been a lot more security around it. The carriages wouldn't have gone missing then.

'So, my girl here will take this away later on. I'll help her load it into the truck after I've come back from lunch. That's why this year there's not too many drinkies for me,' said Davi. 'Got to have a clear head.'

'How does the cold affect the carriage?' asked Emmett.

'It'll be fine; it'll be in the fire station; there'll be no heating on. The coolness will help it because it will acclimatise slowly. I've looked at it,' said Davi. 'It shouldn't be a problem. Hopefully, the horses will be good. You don't want to pull it too hard, nice and steady. It'll look magnificent in the parade. Miss McNeice is looking forward to it. We're always people who like to make Miss McNeice happy, aren't we?'

He turned and looked at Rash. It seemed to Emmett that she almost frowned at him.

'You don't agree with that?' said Emmett.

'What do I care?' said the girl. 'My job is to not to make people happy, just to get it there. Once it's there, I'm done and

I'm off for Christmas Eve. I'll celebrate, go with friends, have a night out, have my dinner tomorrow.'

'Not going down to the parade, then?'

'No,' she said.

'How's it getting back?' asked Emmett.

For a moment, Rash seemed to be deep in thought. Then she shook her shoulders quickly.

'We'll keep it locked up in the fire station,' said Davi. 'A few people round there. We have security hired for it. It's all been done. Don't worry.'

After looking at the carriage for several minutes, Davi locked the room up again before Rash took them out and showed them the truck. She explained the folding level at the back, how they would roll the carriage onto it. The platform would lift up and they'd roll the carriage into the truck. She would secure it down with ties, and then she would make her way down into the town.

Emmett still marvelled at the size of her for driving a truck like that, but she seemed to know what she was talking about. She gave a wave and said goodbye, off to do her Christmas shopping. The time was now approaching seven, but Emmett guessed that meant she was going there early. A few shops were opening up at eight o'clock, and he hadn't any shopping done himself. He had ordered some presents, including one for Sabine, but it would be down in Glasgow.

He wandered back over to Davi, asking what he was going to do prior to his lunch.

'I'll stay here,' said Davi. 'Not much point going home. Sit in the canteen, have coffee, might go down and just do some last checks around the old girl, make sure she's okay. Miss McNeice will want to see her too before she goes on the truck.'

'Maybe it's best that we come back and ride with Rash,' he said.

'You can do. Go into town with her, drop the truck off. She'll be back around about two, three o'clock to do that. I'm heading off for lunch at about half eleven.'

'Sounds good. I think I'll do that.'

Emmett wondered what to do now. He'd been to Hamper Holdings. The carriage was safe. The plan looked good. He was going to accompany the carriage down. At the moment, it couldn't go anywhere. Davi was going to stay here with it, so it wouldn't disappear. It couldn't get out of the compound.

Emmett decided he would go back up and have a coffee. He'd need the caffeine to stay awake because he'd been up all night. His shoulders were tired and his mind wandered to Sabine. Maybe she needed some help.

However, she was busy, and he had his instructions to remain off at Hamper Holdings. As he sat down to drink another cup of coffee, his phone vibrated. Picking it up, he saw it was Clarissa.

'How are you going?' she said, clearly agitated.

'It's here,' said Emmett. 'It looks fine. It's in the lock-up. I'm going to ride with it into Inverness later on. It's not going anywhere.'

'I'm going to head back to the station. Get to the office for round about half eleven, something like that,' said Clarissa.

'Okay,' said Emmett. 'Carriage should be okay. There's also got the security guards on the gate. I'll brief them not to let anybody out. Check all the trucks going in or out.'

'Very good. Make sure that thing doesn't move. But then down to the station, I want to brief about tonight and what we're going to do. I see this as the best chance for it to be stolen at this parade,' said Clarissa. 'I just don't know how they're going to do it. It's so public. It's—'

'We'd better watch the fire station when they drop it off down there,' said Emmett. 'That would be a prime candidate. The quiet hours before things happen.'

'Well, the switch here happened like that. Away from everyone. While there was plenty of noise going on. But the fakes . . .' said Clarissa, making a whoop, 'the fake ones they put up here are good. But they're not that good. Sabine spotted it as it went past. Took her a bit to confirm it, but she spotted it.'

'I probably wouldn't have,' said Emmett.

There was silence on the other end of the phone. 'No, you wouldn't have,' said Clarissa. 'You completely wouldn't have. I'm going to get down there when it gets to the fire station. Make sure there's no jiggery-pokery going on. Make sure the right one's going out on parade tonight. Not going to make that mistake twice.'

'Good,' said Emmett. 'I'll stay here and then I'll see you down at the station. How are things at that end?'

'I'm about to phone Macleod, which means the Chief Constable's going to hear about this. No doubt he'll go bananas. I'll probably get the blame for this, but Lady bloody Angela didn't have any proper security. She's treating these things like they're nothing. She wasn't even happy to have Sabine there.'

'It's not your fault,' said Emmett, 'but we'll get them.'

'You're awfully confident,' said Clarissa.

'Just positive,' said Emmett. 'Just positive.'

'You think we'll catch them in the act?'

'I don't know,' said Emmett. 'I think, well, I don't know what I think at the moment. That's the problem. But something's brewing in my head.'

'Well, if you can brew it quicker,' said Clarissa, 'it'd be much appreciated. Gotta go. I'll see you at the station.'

'Okay.'

Emmett sat and drank his coffee again. Something was brewing in his head. He wasn't sure about Rash. There was something about her. But he would travel with her. He'd go down with her so he would cover that off.

And then they would get to the fire station. Clarissa would be there. She could check the items. The carriage hadn't left Hamper Holdings. Clarissa had been in. She had verified it. It's the right one. This sort of thing couldn't just disappear out.

Emmett looked at his watch. He had a couple of hours; it was time to let his brain think. From his jacket, he pulled out a notepad. Opening it up, there was a sketch of a rather strange-looking creature. He took some colouring pencils out from his pocket and drew, colouring in the shape. It was a painting scheme he was going to use. Sometimes you had to do something else to let the brain expand. He wasn't sure if Clarissa would understand.

Chapter 22

'How on earth did they just waltz in and take it?'

'Why 'they'?' asked Emmett.

'I don't think you're getting the point, Emmett,' said Clarissa. 'How did they waltz in and get it? How do these people not put up proper security? These carriages are valuable.'

'I'm not sure you're getting it,' said Emmett. Clarissa stared at him.

They had come back to the station and were now in a small conference room. Clarissa was on edge. The case was not going well. A case of theft and five items had been stolen. She wasn't any further forward.

'I'm still no further forward with Garrick. Can't find him. Nobody can find him,' said Patterson.

'That's old news, Patterson. What have you got new for me?'

'The family. Lady Angela is a sister to Katie Grouse.'

'You've already told us that,' spat Clarissa.

'I know,' said Patterson. Listen.' He was getting agitated and tempers were starting to rise. In the corner, Sabine shuffled. She was never one to engage in a shouting match.

'Well, what have you got then?' said Clarissa.

'McNeice, who owns Emperor Holdings. She's their mother.'

'What?' said Clarissa. 'What? You're having a laugh.'

'No. I looked into it, pulled family records, and yes, McNeice is their mother.'

'She said "Mater,"' blurted Sabine. 'She said "Mater" on the phone when she was speaking to McNeice. I asked Eric to check it.'

'Come on, people,' said Clarissa suddenly. 'A word to the boss wouldn't have gone amiss. So we've got three of them who own the actual carriages.'

'Three of them, all at a secret auction,' said Emmett suddenly.

'Three of them at a secret auction,' said Clarissa. 'So they went as a family. They had a bit of money together.'

'You think she bought the carriages for the girls beforehand?' asked Sabine. 'Where did Garrett get his? Where did Ursula Knight get hers? Are they both picking them up from an auction?'

'One thing I don't understand,' said Patterson. 'I went into Hamper Holdings and McNeice's involvement. She seems to have come out of nowhere with this business.'

'Women are successful sometimes, you know,' said Clarissa.

'No,' said Patterson. 'The business seemed to have jumped to large-scale straight away. Think about it. You're doing these hampers. It's a new technology. You don't just launch in. You know? It's not ambient goods, but a mix requiring a better way of delivery in the hampers. There's all manner of goods in them. These hampers are done specially. They're delivered so they're fresh. There's a wee bit of technology inside of it. That's a big risk. It's food items as well. So that's serious money you've got to put into their development.'

'What are you getting at?' asked Sabine from the corner.

'Sabine's asking where McNeice got the funding for that?' said Emmett. 'Lo-and-behold, we've got three of them, with four of the carriages.'

'Well, she clearly must have money from somewhere,' said Clarissa.

'But why put it into the carriages?' asked Emmett.

'Because they're an investment, Emmett. Not everyone's an art lover like me,' said Clarissa.

'But she's got investments. She's got the business, so she's got to invest in the business. She's also got to invest in buying these carriages from a secret auction. If you've gone for four, why not go for six? Why not have the whole collection? Shouldn't it be worth more? It's like Monopoly, isn't it?' said Emmett.

'It's like what?' blurted a stunned Clarissa.

'Monopoly,' said Emmett, staring at her, as if the answer was obvious.

'I think what Emmett means is when you buy the houses in Monopoly, they're worth more when somebody lands on them if you own all the properties of that colour,' said Sabine.

'I know how Monopoly works,' said Clarissa. 'These carriages are not like Monopoly. It's just a game.'

'It's all just a game,' said Patterson, almost absentmindedly.

'What?' said Clarissa.

'It's all just a game, don't you see it?'

'No, these items are special, they're magical, they're—'

'Not for some people,' said Emmett. 'Clarissa, boss, listen a moment.'

Clarissa forced herself to try to calm down.

'The thing about this case is you've been looking at this as an art lover. These carriages, they're magnificent, everybody wants to have them, and with some people, that might be true.

Garrick, yes. But whenever we went to these other people, most of them didn't seem to give two stuffs about the actual items, about their preciousness. They're just another heirloom in the corner. They're just another bit to show off on the shelf. Garrick wasn't though. Garrick's just a private man hiding everything.'

'Garrick still could be the one who wants them all,' said Clarissa.

'I don't think so,' said Patterson.

'And why's that?' asked Clarissa.

'Because he's dead.'

'He's what?'

'He's dead. Didn't you get the message? It's just come through to me.'

'What message?'

'It was sent about five or six in the morning. It's Perry. Perry's messaged me. He said that Hope had messaged you.'

Clarissa grabbed her phone out and started looking through. 'Damn thing's not updating. What's going on with this?'

She looked, but nothing made sense. Nothing seemed to have been picked up until recently. There was a message there now. It had been sent at five or six in the morning.

'Bollocks,' said Clarissa. 'I've only just got the message here now. It's only just come in since we've marched in here to have this meeting.'

Sabine walked over towards Clarissa's phone. 'May I?' she asked.

'I know how to work a phone.'

'Everything all right?' said a voice at the door. There'd been no knock, and he'd just opened the door. Macleod stood there.

'Don't you know how to enter a room?' asked Clarissa,

glaring at him.

'Pot, kettle, black,' said Macleod, much to her annoyance. Sabine picked up Clarissa's phone.

'Um, there's something wrong with your SIM card,' she said.

'There's nothing wrong with my SIM card. I got a message from Frank about three hours ago.'

'Frank's on your normal SIM card, yes? We got them swapped over. We keep them separate now, remember? After the Italy thing with Susan, we decided it would be good to have two SIM cards on everyone's phone.'

Clarissa glowered at Sabine. 'What are you saying?'

'Your SIM card. It's corrupted. That's why the message didn't come through.'

'I was going to ask how that was getting on. The difference now you know he's dead.'

'I've only just found out Garrick's dead,' said Clarissa.

'Garrick was the body up on the hillside,' said Macleod, 'with the bracelet.'

'Yes, I know now.'

'So how does that change things?'

'I don't know,' said Clarissa. She sat down, and then she stood up again quickly. 'Sabine, take Pats. Get up to the Cairngorms. Find out what's happening on Garrick's estate. I want to know if Laura Silver knows anything about his death.'

'On our way,' said Sabine. 'I'll message you via your normal SIM.'

Sabine turned and looked at Patterson. He was already grabbing his jacket. Together, they barged out through the door while Macleod stepped aside. Once they'd gone, he looked over at Clarissa.

'So where are we at?'

'Where we're at is, we've got one carriage left that hasn't been stolen. Emmett's going to accompany it. I'll be there later on tonight. We're going to look after it. I think somebody might come for it and I'll grab them then.'

'I thought that was the idea last night.'

'It would have been fine, but Lady Angela was—'

'Don't blame other people. Get your head together,' said Macleod.

Clarissa turned and glared at him.

'Should I leave the room?' asked Emmett.

'No,' said Macleod. 'Get your head together. What do you know?'

'All we know, Seoras, is we've had five carriages taken. Three of them were taken from Lady Angela and Katie Grouse. They're sisters. Their mum is McNeice, who owns Hamper Holdings, and has the last carriage. Garrick, who owned the smallest one, is dead. He hasn't been seen for two months. Laura Silver said he was on the move.'

'And she's lying?'

'Do you think?' said Clarissa.

'Stay calm. And what's next?'

'Laura Silver—she could be in on it,' said Emmett. 'The two ladies, Lady Angela and Katie Grouse, they had flashers turned up at their houses. Didn't think anything of it, just some pervert, except—any description hasn't been of a man, or at least not a man's—'

'Dingle dangles,' said Clarissa.

'What?' said a bemused Macleod.

'Their dingle dangles; they were flashers who never flashed you with, you know—'

'How did they flash, then?' asked Macleod.

'Backside,' said Emmett. 'Wasn't described as a particularly male backside, either.'

'And you think these flashers have got something to do with who stole the items?' asked Macleod.

'At Lady Angela's, there were three men meant to be bringing in the two carriages. One of them was a young lad. He got knocked out, put in the back of a truck. However, when the men came out, they say they saw him in the front. Now, he's a young lad. If you're a woman, you could play a young lad. Especially if—'

'What?' asked Macleod.

'Especially if you're . . . well, you don't look like a, well, what we would define as woman. You're more androgynous. Closer to that sort of in-between type of look.'

'And who is this person?' asked Macleod.

'Probably Laura Silver, isn't it? Whoever she is,' said Emmett.

'Well, in that case, we're all right,' said Clarissa. 'Sabine's on her way to pick her up. Message her. Who knows if my phone will talk to her?'

* * *

As they raced out of Inverness, Patterson at the wheel, Sabine received a message on her phone from Emmett.

'Bring Laura Silver in for questioning,' it said. 'Believe she has something to do with all of this.'

'What's that?' asked Patterson.

'They said we should bring Laura Silver in. I was going to do it, anyway.'

'Snow's getting worse tonight, isn't it? You think this parade's going to go on okay?'

'Well, the way it's falling now, and it's Christmas Eve. It's a big parade. I mean, you want snow, don't you?' said Sabine. 'I'll tell you something; it'll be Baltic.'

Snow was coming down in heavy flurries. Patterson turned the car up towards the small estate that was owned by Garrick. As they arrived at the gate, there was nobody to answer. Sabine unhitched it, and they drove the car up to the front door.

She rang the doorbell, but no one answered. If Laura Silver had been there, she'd have come out to meet them. Sabine tried the door. It turned and opened of its own accord.

'I know they're all about making things not appear to be a place that holds expensive items, but very few people leave their doors open like this.'

'Let's look inside, then,' said Patterson.

Sabine and Patterson walked through the house. They went back and found the security cameras and the room where they'd previously watched the footage. They played it back and Laura Silver had been there a couple of days before, but there'd been none of her recently.

As they walked around, Patterson turned to Sabine. 'When we were here previously, there seemed to be a lot more items here.'

'Really,' said Sabine, 'what sort of items?'

'A few gold, some sort of silver ones. When we were sitting up here, it was—well, actually hang on, might still be on the video footage. It has the living room.'

They went back and played the video footage, and Sabine looked at the items that Patterson was now pointing out that had disappeared. She tried to blow the screen up to get a closer look. It wasn't their own system, so it took time. But as she did so, she spotted something.

'I can't say,' said Sabine, 'because I don't have the actual item. But if I'm honest, some of those look quite expensive. Like proper expensive. Like hide-away-somewhere expensive and not put-on-show expensive. That's very Garrick, I would think.'

'But they're gone.'

'Indeed they are. I wonder why.'

'Laura Silver's gone, too,' said Patterson.

'That she is. Getting herself a little nest egg for leaving, do you think?'

'Why would you need a nest egg,' said Patterson, 'if you had the carriages?'

'Some of these other items might be easier to move on. Carriages are what we're looking for. It's only your keen eyes that have spotted that these things aren't here. Otherwise, anyone coming in wouldn't know.'

'Garrick's not keeping an inventory. He's not around anymore to quibble,' said Patterson.

'So, Laura Silver's on the run. She's done a flyer.'

'If she's the one picking these carriages up, if she's the one that's hoarding them, I think the other one will go tonight, then. She's not going to hang around for much longer, is she?' said Patterson. 'And after that, it's going back to storage after the parade. Now is the time when it's on the move.'

'She seems to have captured the last lot when they've been on the move. She obviously decided it was too difficult to get into Lady Angela's house. I can understand that,' said Sabine, 'because it was pretty well guarded. So she did it at her friend's, with security that's not understanding what it's trying to protect, how to protect it.'

'But Hamper Holdings, they've got the last one.'

'It's in the lock-up. Somebody's with it. Emmett said he was going to stay with it. It can't go out through the gate as they've got security.'

'We'll be all right then, won't we?' said Patterson.

'Maybe,' said Sabine. 'What we do know is that this will be our chance to get her. She'll make a move for it at some point, so we need to stay on top of that. That's what we need to do. Be on top of that. Grab her when she comes for it. Hope will want her as well. She may be up for murder.'

'Oh well. Do you want to ring Clarissa or me?' asked Patterson. 'At least we know who it is. And we know how we're going to catch her. Might make her a bit happier.'

'Fat chance,' said Sabine. 'The only thing that'll make her happy is seeing Laura Silver behind bars. Until then, we're all going to get an earful.'

Chapter 23

Emmett was making his way back to Hamper Holdings, ready to oversee the transfer of the carriage down for the procession that night. It was snowing heavily now, but he was happy because he had his new gloves with him. They were thick, warm, and with his barbarian-logo beanie hat, he'd be snug enough.

He arrived back at Hamper Holdings in plenty of time, and before Davi and Rash had got there. It was about twenty minutes later when Davi came up into the canteen and spotted Emmett, inviting him down, saying they were going to do the loading. Emmett thanked him and followed him, and found Rash standing outside the room where the carriage was currently secured in. With a quick turn of his hand, Davi set the code, opened up the door, and Emmett breathed a sigh of relief as he saw the carriage still there. At least nothing had gone wrong so far.

He then stood at the rear of the facility, watching as Rash loaded her van, and Davi with a couple of other men, pushed the carriage out.

'You could move it on your own. It would roll easy enough. You could push it,' said Davi, 'but best if we have several of us around it. Just in case there's a slip, we don't want to damage it.'

'Absolutely not,' said Emmett. 'It really looks something.'

Carefully, the men, under Davi's instruction, rolled the carriage onto the rear platform of the lorry. The platform was lifted, and the item then pushed into the back of the lorry before being secured. Rash closed the lorry up and then sat in the front seat of it, preparing to drive off. Emmett advised he would follow down in the car so he would have it with him, when Davi said he would jump into the lorry.

'The girl's done good,' said Davi. 'You can always trust my girl.'

One man who was assisting turned round to Emmett. 'It's a bit off, isn't it, the way he says that? He been saying that she's his girl since she came round originally to talk about this and the plant—'

'Maybe it's just a saying,' said Emmett. 'You know, old guys get like that. Probably nothing in it.'

The man, who was maybe in his forties, turned and looked at him. 'If he treated my daughter like that, I'd be all over him.'

'Like what?' asked Emmett.

'Well, I think there's something going on between them.'

'What?'

'I swore one time I walked in and he was giving her a cuddle.'

'A cuddle?' queried Emmett.

'Yes, a cuddle.'

Emmett thought for a moment. 'Anything else beyond a cuddle?' he said.

'Well, I didn't see anything else, but, you know, you don't do that, do you? You don't cuddle a girl that age when you're his age. Dirty old fella.'

'But you saw nothing beyond it.'

'No,' he said.

'And she's never said anything to you, or asked any of you to step in?' asked Emmett.

'No, well, I didn't say anything. Didn't think it was my place. She might be, well, she might be one of those women into old men. But in my experience, I've never had a twenty-year-old come up to me and ask to jump in my cab.'

Emmett looked at the man and all he could think was, *no, you probably haven't.*

'Well, thanks for that information,' said Emmett. He turned away, and Davi shouted over at him.

'Are you ready? I'm just going to get in the cab and we'll go.'

'Give me two minutes,' said Emmett. 'I just need to phone the station to advise them.'

Emmett picked up the phone and called Patterson. He was on his way back from the Cairngorms. They'd sent forensics out to Garrick's abode for two reasons: one, for the murder team, in case there was any evidence there; but also, to see if they could pick up any clues to the identity of Laura Silver. Had she been involved in previous crimes?

'Eric,' said Emmett to Patterson. 'Do me a favour. When you get back to the station, look into Oliver Davitt.'

'Oliver Davitt? Who's that then?'

'He's the guy who's looking after the carriage.'

'Really? I thought the secret auction was run by someone with a similar name. Wasn't there a signature on it?'

'Couldn't make the signature out. It's a secret auction. But it is signed off as being bought legitimately.'

'I'm going to look at that signature again,' said Patterson. 'I know we couldn't say who it was.'

'That's the whole point of signatures, isn't it? Especially at a secret auction.'

'What's the guy's name?'

'He calls himself Davi,' said Emmett. 'But really, he's Davitt. Oliver Davitt.'

'I've seen that name somewhere before,' said Patterson. 'When I get back, I'll look it up for you. What are you wanting from me about him?'

'See if he's got any family.'

Emmett gave a nod over to Davi, and the lorry pulled off with Emmett in tow. The drive down into Inverness was busy but uneventful, the lorry pulling up on the old fire station grounds. Emmett watched as Davi, with several men, took the carriage off the lorry and stowed it inside the firehouse. He then waved bye-bye to Rash, who took her lorry and drove off.

Emmett stood inside the firehouse, awaiting Clarissa. She said she would join him and from then on, they wouldn't leave the carriage's side. As they were waiting, he turned to Davi. He was wiping down the carriage.

'You got any family?'

'Oh, don't talk to me about families,' he said. And the man said nothing else.

'Have you got family?' Emmett repeated.

'Told you I did. Just don't talk to me about them.'

'Sons?'

'Sons would have been better.'

'Girls then?'

'Yes,' said Davi. He said nothing else as he continued to clean.

'So you've got a girl somewhere? You're married?'

'I am married,' said the man.

He clearly wasn't for saying any more, and Emmett was trying to judge the mood of the man. He needed to elicit some information. Well, Patterson was looking it up anyway, so maybe that was a better route to achieve his aims.

The door opened and Emmett could tell from the way it opened that Clarissa had arrived. She bounded into the fire station bay, looking around her.

'All here safe and sound,' said Emmett.

Clarissa marched over to him, gave a small nod, and then looked to her left at the carriage.

'What the hell?' she said.

'What's wrong?' said Emmett.

'That's not the carriage. That's a fake,' said Clarissa. She marched up to the wheels and touched them. She looked around it. 'It's a hell of a fake, but it's a fake,' she said. 'Davi, how do you not know this is a fake?'

The man did not respond, but instead continued to wipe down part of the carriage. He was whistling.

'I spoke to you,' she said.

'I'm not sure he's all there,' said Emmett.

'It'll be ready soon,' said Davi.

'Emmett, this is the wrong thing. This is not the carriage. Where is it?'

'It was there this morning. I didn't leave except for our meeting,' he said.

His phone was ringing in his pocket. He reached for it, but Clarissa turned to him.

'There's no time for a phone call. We've got to work out where this went.'

'Well, I followed it down the entire way here. I didn't lose sight of it. So that carriage was the one that was in Hamper

Holdings.'

'I saw the one in Hamper Holdings. The one in Hamper Holdings was the real thing.'

'But there wasn't another one that came in,' said Emmett. 'That's the one that left. I was in the room and that's the one that left.'

Clarissa turned and grabbed Davi. 'Where's the carriage?'

'It's here,' he said. 'This is the carriage. It's lovely, isn't it?'

She stared at him and then turned to see Emmett on his phone.

'I told you, there's no time for the phone. Listen—'

'Wait a minute,' said Emmett, putting his hand up in front of Clarissa. She nearly reached to snap it off.

'We need to act,' said Clarissa.

'We need to know where to act,' said Emmett. 'Patterson's just looked something up. Oliver!' The man didn't flinch as he was cleaning the carriage.

'Davi, you mean,' said Clarissa.

'Oliver Davitt,' said Emmett. 'Patterson reckons your secret auction signature could be Oliver Davitt. It's very unclear. But Oliver Davitt has a daughter. Oliver Davitt had a first wife. The first wife died. Oliver Davitt then, according to Patterson, he married Miss McNeice. Miss McNeice is not Miss McNeice. That was her maiden name. Her correct name is Mrs Isabel Davitt. And she's married to that man there.'

'Why the heck didn't they tell us? And why is he working like this?' asked Clarissa.

'Davi, where's your daughter?' asked Emmett.

The man slowed down his cleaning.

'Davi, I said, where's your daughter? What's she called?'

'You have a daughter, sir,' said Clarissa to the man. She

grabbed his shoulder, shaking him, but he just tensed.

'I have several daughters,' he said.

'He's got two stepdaughters,' said Emmett.

'Hang on a minute,' said Clarissa. 'You're telling me he owned all the carriages at one point?'

'So it would seem.'

'And his step wife owns the biggest one, and his two stepdaughters own two of the others. What the hell's Garrick doing with it? And Ursula Knight?'

'I was wondering,' said Emmett. 'How much do you think those carriages would have been worth selling on the quiet? Enough to get a good business going? A lot of investment went into it, as far as I believe.'

'So who's coming for the carriages now?' shouted Clarissa.

'I think Mr Davitt had a child in the beginning.'

'And you think this child is who—?'

'Remind me,' said Emmett suddenly. 'Laura Silver. In the report somewhere. You said how she was dressed. You said there was something remarkable about her dress. Wasn't your type of thing, but you thought it was—'

'She wore a coat full of rushes.' Clarissa corrected, 'made from rushes.'

'And how did she look?'

'Petite, small frame, little androgynous, black hair, more like a mop on her head than a fine sort of hanging hair.'

'Rash,' said Emmett suddenly. 'Rash, hair out the back, didn't hang like a proper ponytail, was thicker, was more bunched. Height, what height was Laura Silver?'

'Five, what, five-four to five-five?'

Emmett picked up the phone, calling back to Patterson. 'Eric, reports of the flashers, look them up. What height were they?'

'Anything from five feet three to about five feet six. A couple of different ideas from different witnesses.'

'It's her,' said Emmett. 'It's her. Rash. Rashin.'

Clarissa turned and looked at him. 'What are you on about? Rashin?'

'Rashin Coatie,' said Emmett. 'Scotland's Cinderella. It's the original. The heroine. Cinderella, her Rashin Coatie, she wears this coat of rushes instead of cinders. Everything taken away from her.'

'Taken away,' said Davi, 'but this time she gets it back.'

'You see, the carriage becomes a pumpkin,' said Emmett. 'Becomes nothing in the original.'

'What?' blurted Clarissa.

'She's taken them back,' said Emmett. 'She's taken back what she believes belongs to her and her father.' He turned and grabbed Davi.

'She told me I'm not strong, but told me to just keep going. Said she would get it back, all of it. It's my girl, my girl! My girl looked after me!'

The man sat down, and Emmett wasn't sure if he was crying or half-smiling.

'Isabel, so cruel, cruel to her, cruel to my Emma.'

'Emma?' said Clarissa, a little perplexed.

'Emma Davitt. It's his daughter from the first marriage.'

'My only girl. Isabel's girls are not mine.'

'Whoa,' said Clarissa. 'What are we saying here?'

'He had a daughter and his wife died. He married Isabel McNeice. Isabel McNeice took the carriages off him, made him sign them over in some secret auction, or at least sign the paperwork to make it look like it was. She gave some to her daughters, one to herself, and sold two others. Two sold to people who will never bring them to light for the money to start up her business, Hamper Holdings. She mustn't have given anything to Emma. At some point, Emma must have been cast out. Whatever happened, Emma's back.'

'They sent my girl away. Put my girl away. She found me, though. She found me,' said Davi.

'So where are the coaches, then?' asked Clarissa.

'Emma's collected them. Emma's done the stealing. And Emma's going to get rid of them.'

'What?' said Clarissa. 'She can't destroy them.'

'But she's not got the capacity to move them on. What better way? You said that these carriages were worth a lot. Sell one or sell two? If you sold one, you'd have enough to start a company, wouldn't you?'

'Well, yes,' said Clarissa.

'So you sell the second for what? For when you make an arse of it? Maybe she's making an arse of it again. Did we check the company? Did we look into it deep enough?' asked Emmett.

'How do we find her?' asked Clarissa.

'Davi, where's Emma live?' said Emmett.

'Hell with that,' said Clarissa. 'Why don't you put your arms up, sir? I'm going to search you.'

Davi just did as he was told, and Clarissa found his wallet inside. 'I'm opening your wallet. I'm not touching your money,' she said.

Tucked away inside, she found a piece of paper. It said 'Rash' with a phone number, and underneath, an address.

'Get Sabine and get Patterson on the go, and then we get in my car,' said Clarissa. 'We might save them if we hurry.'

Chapter 24

There were loud noises and horns being sounded, and probably a lot of swearing somewhere. The car raced along the Inverness roads thick with snow and Christmas traffic.

'It's only carriages,' said Emmett. 'It's just stuff.'

'It's not stuff. It's art. It's proper art. And it's art worth saving. Now shut up and tell me where I'm going.'

Emmett found his boss rather chaotic, and Emmett was not a chaotic man. Despite this, he held his cool and advised the next turn.

'It appears she's out in the middle of almost nowhere. There's a quarry.'

'A quarry?' said Clarissa. 'She's surely not going to dump it in a quarry?'

'It's an old one, not used anymore. It's mainly covered in. From what I can see from the satellite photograph, there's a lot of grass in it, but it's a steep drop. These carriages are pretty delicate, aren't they?'

'They're a work of art. You don't bounce them along the road,' said Clarissa.

Emmett swore the car went faster, even though he wasn't

sure how.

'Take a left,' said Emmett. 'I think there's a shortcut.'

'A shortcut? How much of a shortcut?' shouted Clarissa over the noise of traffic and the car engine.

'I can cut five miles off the route. I told you, she's in the middle of nowhere, but there's a track that heads that way. You think this car's up to it?'

'Course it is,' said Clarissa.

Emmett directed her off the A9, outside of Inverness, and along a small side road. Snow was falling heavily. The road was slippery, and Clarissa was going full tilt. The only thing that Emmett was thankful for was that the snow had begun long before they got in the car, so the hood was up. However, the windows were down, Clarissa at times leaning out to see properly through the driving snow.

'Next left off here,' said Emmett.

Clarissa spun the car, turned and hit the brakes. The back end of the car slid as she pulled the handbrake, and she stopped inches before a gate.

'You never said there was a gate!'

But Emmett was already out of the car, opening the gate as Clarissa drove through. Emmett closed it behind them before jumping back in the car.

'Along here,' he said.

Clarissa looked in front of her. 'Where?'

'There's a road here, there's a path. There's something solid underneath. Go!'

Clarissa almost took it as a challenge. The wheels of the car spun briefly before the car was off. As they turned another corner, in through a wooded glade, the snow gave way to a path. The corners were tight, and Clarissa was driving as fast as she could, swinging the car this way and that. As she cleared the wood, she turned to Emmett.

'Macleod's paying for a proper bloody clean on this thing. Where now?'

'Over there,' he said. 'That's the top of the hill. I believe there are buildings on the other side of it.'

'It's just a field, isn't it?'

'Don't go along the bottom of it. Go up by the hedge.'

'Why?' she asked.

'Because the drift's been coming that way. That hedge is protecting it. The thinnest snow is going to be beside the hedge.'

'But where's the path go?'

'I don't know. It goes across the field,' said Emmett. 'I can't see it because of the snow.'

Clarissa spun the car up the side, following the hedgerow up to the top. She then turned left and followed the hedge along until it came out through another gate that Emmett had to open. It was only another two hundred feet after that until they crested the hill. Sure enough, over on the left-hand side was a small cottage. Beyond the cottage was a barn, and Clarissa made for it.

The car stopped and Clarissa jumped out, looking around.

'Where is it? It'll be in the barn, won't it?' she said, and began running towards it. Emmett was hurrying after her, because Clarissa was like a woman possessed. She pulled down a latch, slid back bolts, and opened the barn doors.

'There's nothing here,' she said. 'There's bloody nothing here.' She walked forward to the rear of the barn, opening those doors. As she did so, she saw on the ground two thin tracks that then ran away from the barn.

'Back in the car,' she said. 'She's taken it this way.'

'She's taken it out?' blurted Emmett.

'Where's that quarry?' said Clarissa.

Emmett jumped back into the car, looking at his map. 'Over that way. Over there.'

Clarissa began driving, following the tracks as best she could. The snow was still coming down heavily, threatening to cover them up, but she reckoned that if the carriage had made it along this way, the car could too. Soon she pulled up, seeing a horse attached to the carriage. The largest carriage looked magnificent even in the snow, but there was a white side to it where the snow had stuck to the side.

Clarissa was in shock that anyone would have such an item out in this snow at this time, but more so now that she saw the quarry beyond. It may have normally been filled with grass, but the quarry was white, the proceeding days of snow forming a white blanket.

The horse was in front of the carriage, but it looked as if it had been removed from the reins that held it to the carriage. Slowly the large animal was being taken round and walked away from the carriage. A small woman was atop the horse.

'Emma Davitt, don't do it!' shouted Emmett. 'There's nowhere to go!'

'They won't have it! These will be worth nothing when I send them down there. It drops, you know that? A massive drop. It'll bounce down and then it'll tip. All the way over the edge. You can tell Davi I did it. Did it for him. Tell Da!'

She jumped off the horse. Clarissa was only twenty feet away, but she saw what the woman was going to do. Emma's shoulder was put to the cart, which was facing down into the quarry. She pushed, and Clarissa saw the carriage move.

'No!' shouted Clarissa.

She tore off towards it, running at full tilt as Emma Davitt mounted the horse again, laughing at the rolling carriage. Emmett tried to push the snow from his eyes, following Clarissa, but he wasn't as quick as her. She was like a woman possessed as she grabbed the back of the carriage, but its momentum had picked up and she couldn't hold it. The carriage trundled down the slope, and Clarissa found her dragging feet unable to stop it.

'Let it go!' shouted Emmett. 'Let it go! It's not worth it!'

'I can get it! Give me a hand!'

But the carriage was rolling now. Clarissa was running to keep up with it, her hands still holding on. She could feel the momentum picking up and she wouldn't be able to hold on like this. Soon her feet would fail her. She'd fall flat in the snow and the carriage would be gone.

Desperately, she swung one leg up. It just about held on to part of the wood. She reached up with her left hand, clawed on to the back of the carriage, pulled tight. Her other knee got up and found some purchase as the carriage bounded along through the snow, the thin wheels cutting their way through. Briefly, Clarissa looked behind her, where Emmett was failing to keep up.

'Jump!' he yelled. 'Jump, you stupid woman!'

Clarissa wasn't jumping, not yet. She pulled hard and then desperately clung tightly as the carriage swung back and forth. She clambered through the rear hole under the canopy, and fell into the rear seat of the carriage. The jewel that was sitting there tumbled forward. Her feet swung in, but hit something hard. She suddenly realised that the second largest carriage was sitting in the carriage.

For a moment, she could see them all—one carriage inside of the other down to the smallest one that you could hold in the palm of your hand. Then her eyes looked up ahead. There was snow, but the snow seemed to drop a long way down.

Quickly, she tried to climb forward. She was being bounced here and there, a hand reaching out to grab the side. Her foot jammed suddenly, and she fell to the floor, and she clocked a long piece of wood sticking up beside the wheel.

Of course. That was the stay that help the coach in place when stationary. But you put it in once it had come to a halt. You didn't just jam it in.

A jolt made her fall backwards. Emmett's voice could be heard in the background.

'Get off, you bloody woman! Get off!'

Clarissa fought her way forward, past each jolt. Ahead of her, she could see the wooden pole sticking up. If she pulled it back, it might just jam the wheel. It might just turn it some way. If she could turn it—well, who knew?

Desperately, she flung herself forward. She collapsed against the front of the pole. It couldn't fall forward, instead being held by a piece of wood. She hooked one of her feet into a corner of the carriage, and with all her strength, she pulled back.

The stay came back, and caught the wheel. There was a loud crack, but the stay had done its job. For a brief moment, the wheel stopped. The momentum pushed forward, and the carriage swung off to the left, and then turned and tipped.

It rolled, spinning over and over, Clarissa trapped inside, before coming to an abrupt halt. As it did so, she was thrown out of the carriage, out into the snow.

'Clarissa!' shouted a voice. 'Clarissa, are you all right?'

She could feel the cold against her cheek, the snow inside her left ear. Her shoulder was aching, having taken the brunt of the jolt she had caused, which turned the carriage over. When she'd been thrown, the landing had been remarkably comfortable, considering. Her foot was sore, though. When it was trapped, she had done something to it, and she wasn't sure what.

'Are you all right?' said Emmett as he got closer. He flung himself down on his knees, and his face came close to hers.

She twisted her head and looked up at him. 'Did you get her?' said Clarissa.

'Oh, you're all right then,' said Emmett. He stood up and looked. 'She was off on the horse,' he said.

'I think I broke some of it,' said Clarissa. 'I think I actually broke some of it. I hope they can fix it.'

'You're a bloody idiot,' said Emmett. 'This stuff isn't worth it. It's just art. It's just something somebody made.'

Clarissa moved herself up onto her elbows, and from there she was able to flip herself onto her back. Her tartan shawl was keeping the cold from her shoulders, but her backside was now in the snow, and the trousers were letting the cold through. She laughed to the sky.

'What?' said Emmett. 'What on earth is funny about this?'

'You do not understand art, do you?' laughed Clarissa. And then she smiled at him. 'I got them. I got them all. Tell Macleod that he can tell the Chief Constable he can come and pick the pieces up whenever he's ready.' She tried to sit up but fell backwards laughing.

Emmett stood up. 'You're crackers,' he said. 'Absolutely crackers.'

'Do something for me,' said Clarissa.

'Apart from calling an ambulance?' said Emmett, already picking his phone up.

'Phone Frank first. Tell him I'll be home tonight. Tell him I want my cuddle.'

Emmett shook his head. 'You can tell him yourself.'

'He won't believe you,' said Clarissa. 'He'll think I'm still with the carriages.'

Emmett gave an exasperated breath. 'Crackers, woman. Just crackers.'

Chapter 25

'Well, thank God for snow,' said Frank. Clarissa looked up at him, standing by her bed.

'Some man took me home last night,' said Clarissa. 'Took off all my clothes and put me into a bed. He even carried me up the stairs.'

'And now his back's paying for it,' said Frank.

She threw a punch and dabbed him the arm.

'Oi,' she said. 'Emmett's not happy with me.'

'Emmett's not happy with you,' said Frank. 'I'm not happy with you. Since when do you go chasing down carriages and jumping in them. You could have got killed.'

'That's a relic. All six of them went together. Six relics. Six fine items of art, Frank,' said Clarissa.

'Seven,' said Frank. 'And the finest one was thrown clear.' She looked up at him. He wasn't joking, though.

'Sorry,' she said. 'I'm not used to thinking about others when I put myself on the line.'

'I know, and you're doing it for the right reasons,' said Frank, 'but don't. Emmett was right. It was the wrong call.'

'I saved them, though, didn't I?'

'This time,' said Frank. 'I don't know. I don't know if they'll be able to be put back together anyway,' he said.

She looked shocked. 'Who said that?'

'Seoras, when he rang.'

'What does he know? It was nothing. They'll be fine.'

'Anyway, you're getting up soon,' said Frank.

'Why?' she asked.

'Christmas Day. Christmas lunch?'

'Do you mind if we just have it here? Bring it in. We'll eat off a tray together here, Frank. It's all I need.'

'I don't mind that, but everybody else might get annoyed.'

'Why?'

'Macleod invited everybody round,' said Frank. 'Said everyone was working hard, was all over the place, so we're all going to his, at least for the afternoon.'

'Seriously?'

'Yes,' said Frank. 'I said if you were up to it. I mean, I could always go and—'

'No, no, we need to go,' she said. 'I'm a bit sore, but we need to go. Besides, it'll do us good, bit of fun, a few drinks. I'll drive over though,' she said.

'No, you won't. He's ordered taxis, anyway.'

'He's ordered taxis?' queried Clarissa. 'What did he do, sell the carriages after I saved them?'

'Chief Constable's paying for yours, apparently.'

Clarissa smiled. 'That's a good sign, at least. I'll have a rest until I have to move.'

'The bath's run. You can have half an hour in it, and then we'll have to get ready.'

'Have you got my . . .'

'The festive trousers? Yes. They're done. There's a sprig of holly for your shawl as well.'

'Come here a minute,' she said.

Frank bent over, and Clarissa flung her arms around him, pulling him close, kissing him deeply. When she let him go, she said, 'You are one in a million, you. Do you know that?'

'So are you,' he said, once again serious. 'Don't do that to me.' She nodded.

It was an hour later when they were in the taxi, making their way across Inverness, out to the Black Isle. Macleod's house sat nestled in amongst the trees with a view out to the Moray Firth. It was thick with snow on the way over, and the trees around Macleod's were lined with it. Underneath was thinner, the trees giving protection from the snow that drifted in.

As Clarissa stepped out of the car, Frank was there to take her arm, leaving the taxi behind as they approached the front door. Frank had a bag in his hand.

'What's that?' she said.

'It's only polite to bring something if somebody's giving you dinner,' he said.

'You thought of everything, didn't you?'

'Well, I've thought of what I've thought of. Who knows if it's everything?'

There was a shout from behind them. 'Merry Christmas!'

The thick Northern Irish accent told Clarissa who it was. She turned to see Emmett and Sabine almost half-running up the drive. She looked over at Emmett's jumper. It was one of those festive ones, but it had some sort of a female warrior on the front, dressed in a snow hat. Clarissa wasn't too sure about what the woman was wearing. There was nothing rude about it; it just didn't look adequate for the snows that surrounded her in the picture.

'How you feeling?' asked Sabine.

'I'm fine,' she said. 'Bit of bruising and that. Since we got back from the hospital, this one here has been making me take it easy. I take it things are all right at the other end?'

'Hope charged her last night with murder. She's been held for the theft as well. We're taking it easy today. Back in tomorrow.'

'I'll get in as well, then.'

'Macleod says no,' said Sabine. 'He said I have to take charge of it.'

'I'm fine, okay?'

'He said you were on holiday. He said it's done and dusted, and I can take the rest of it. And he's right. He's put me and Emmett up in a better hotel, anyway.'

'Okay. Well, we'll see about that,' she said, as the door opened. Standing there in a crisp white shirt and a festive tie was Macleod. He looked very out of sorts in the tie, but he gave her a hard stare.

'Are you all right?'

'I wish everyone would stop fussing. I'm fine.'

'Good. Then you can come in. No twister for you, though.'

She heard Sabine and Emmett snigger behind her.

'That's only because I've kicked your backside last time,' said Clarissa, walking in.

Macleod shook Frank's hand as he entered, welcoming him to the house.

'Everyone's here,' he said, 'except Ross. Ross is having a family day. He'll drop by later this evening. You can stay as long as you want. I don't want to hold anybody back from any personal time they're wanting, but I thought you could do with feeding. Didn't give you a lot of chance to organise Christmas.'

Macleod took Clarissa's shawl from her, hung up everyone's coats, and they made their way through into the living room. Buck's Fizz was passed around, with Macleod having a sparkling orange juice. There was a seat by the fire for Clarissa. She scolded him, saying she wasn't a grandmother, to which he said she was the nearest thing he had in the building.

As everyone settled into chatting, Macleod knelt down beside Clarissa's chair. He fixed her with a serious stare.

'You did well,' he said. 'I'm going to take an officer away from you, possibly two. You'll get some new people. You'll be involved in choosing them. The Chief Constable's giving me a remit to form a new unit.'

'You can't do that. Do I get to know who you're taking from me?'

'Well, I'm not taking Patterson. He's the only one who can truly handle you.' Macleod gave a smile.

'Sabine?' Clarissa whispered. 'Why Sabine?'

'Sabine needs to spread her wings. Do some different stuff. She's good. She's very good but also very young. I don't want her to sit underneath you for the next lot of years. I want her to spread her wings, to see more. She can come back then when you finally hang your shawl up.'

'I'll need some people who understand their art. It nearly cost us this time. Emmett doesn't know his art. I'd have stopped this thing happening if it had been me at Hamper Holdings.'

'Emmett's the one I want to move.'

Clarissa sat and thought for a moment. 'You're right. He's good. He's very good. Why is he—'

'Emmett doesn't fit in,' said Macleod. 'He's not a macho detective. He's not a fundamental, by-the-book detective. Did you know he paints little men? He disappears off for role-playing games. He is probably better suited to things that are a little more quirky. Things that the rest of us can't get our heads around.'

'You're saying he's better suited to things that you can't get your head around. That's quite a compliment,' said Clarissa.

'He doesn't know yet. Neither does Sabine. I'm going to offer him Sabine as his deputy. She's not experienced enough to move up to inspector, but with him she'll get a lot of experience if she accepts. If she doesn't, she'll sit in the arts division with you. You've seen a lot; you've been in different places in this force—she hasn't. She needs to go to them.'

'When do I get to choose my new ones?'

'As soon as they accept, you can start hunting through the entire force out there. You get to hire them. I can't expand your division at the moment. Base them where you want, but you'll have to cover Glasgow.'

'That's okay.'

'And one more thing,' he said.

'What's that?' said Clarissa.

'I know you love your art. I know you think it's beyond price. None of my officers are. Hope jumped off into a river, getting a detonator device away from a man who was going to blow up a dam and kill people. That's a good sacrifice, if there ever is one. You, however, would have killed yourself for stuff. They're just things.'

'This is why you've never been in the arts division. This is why I have questions about whether or not you should head it up,' said Clarissa.

'We risk ourselves to save others, not to save stuff,' said Macleod, seriously.

'It was my call, and I made it. Is everything wrapped up with it, though?'

'It will be,' said Macleod. 'I feel sorry for Emma Davitt. Apparently, she was a happy little girl with her father, Davi, as they called him at Humber Holdings. Her mother died, and then when he married her stepmother, she had two older sisters. They weren't very nice to her. It seemed that McNeice used her father and the carriages that he owned to set herself up in business. Garrick and Ursula Knight bought the smaller ones off her.

'The company was in trouble again, though. But I think Emma did it out of spite. She wanted to take back what wasn't theirs, and she was going to destroy it so they couldn't get it again. She was clever in her own way. I would have a lot of sympathy for her,' said Macleod, 'except for one thing.'

'She killed Garrick, didn't she? I know. Ursula Knight—'

'Ursula Knight's missing. We've contacted her people since, the correct people. Emmett's theory or ideas about this androgynous person were correct. Emma was Laura Silver, also Felix Rastrum. She worked it because she never had to be about the whole time, based in Scotland looking after the houses. She was also the flasher, which is why—'

'No dingle-dangle,' said Clarissa, almost laughing.

'But she killed both of them. She had no need to, she could have stolen the stuff—'

'She couldn't have stolen it and got away with it and covered it up,' said Clarissa. 'Nobody knew they were missing except her and her would-be employers who were already dead. That's how she stole those two carriages easily.'

'Not strictly accurate,' said Macleod. 'The theft from Garrick she did while he was alive. When he went to the Chief Constable, she realised there was a flaw. We were already involved at that point, so she killed him before we even arrived. Buried him out in the Cairngorms, but as fate would have it, a dog, out with its master, found him. Found the bracelet through which we traced him.

'He was a proper collector, as you would have it. Dark, seedy character, though, and a rough one,' said Macleod.

'So that's it,' she said. 'Case closed.'

'Not quite. Trying to work out what to do with Oliver Davitt. He's an accomplice in some ways, although I'm not sure he understood everything. Trying to work out his mental state, but that'll be for somebody else, not me. We'll see what the Procurator Fiscal says about it all. But we've done well. The Chief Constable's happy. Items are recovered. Murder's solved. I think we deserve Christmas.'

'I think we do.'

As Macleod stood up, Clarissa looked round at Hope. She was there, standing beside her partner John; there was a glow about her and she gave Clarissa a wave. Only Als was missing and Clarissa felt that loss. She had great affection for Als, similar to Pats. It was part of enjoying being in the force, working with people like that—people who could roll with her.

She watched as Macleod walked over to Emmett, taking him to one side. It was hard to read Emmett's face, as Macleod was obviously putting a proposition to him. A few minutes later, she saw Emmett talking to Sabine. There was a smile on Sabine's face.

Clarissa would be sad to lose her, but in truth, Macleod was right. She needed to develop, and she would not do that with Clarissa. She wondered about Macleod. He was giving her a new team, bringing people on. She realised the vote of confidence he had in her, trusting her with new people. Not just someone who had experience in the job, like Sabine or Emmett. A whole new team.

She needed somebody who could chase down items though. She looked over at Perry. Not someone like Perry, though. She and Perry were the same. She needed different people on her team. People who weren't hotheads, rash, and who charged into the fray. People who could be taught the dirty side of fighting if need be. Maybe someone who could actually fight if they had call for it.

Frank knelt down beside her. 'Why so restless?'

'He's given me my Christmas present.'

'Which was?'

'My own team.'

'I thought he'd already done that.'

'Oh no. This time he's really given me my team.' Clarissa smiled, and Frank snaked an arm around her, giving her a kiss on the cheek.

'As long as you're happy,' he said.

She turned and looked at him. 'I won't be going in,' she said. 'Sabine will handle the wrap-up stuff. I'm meant to be off these couple of weeks. We're going to start again. Tomorrow, we will start our Christmas holiday, you and me. You deserve it, Frank.'

'I'll believe that when I see it,' he said. He wasn't angry.

She reached forward and took his hands. 'I'm sorry.'

'Sorry for what?' he said.

'Charging down that hill in that carriage. Charging out of the coffee shop when we were on our break. Not even seeing if anybody else could take it.'

'I knew who you were when I married you. I married you

for a reason.'

She leaned over, giving Frank a hug. Looking beyond him, she saw Macleod, with Jane hugging him close. She saw Macleod glance over at her, and she simply whispered the words, 'Thank you.'

He mouthed back, 'Merry Christmas.'

Read on to discover the Patrick Smythe series!

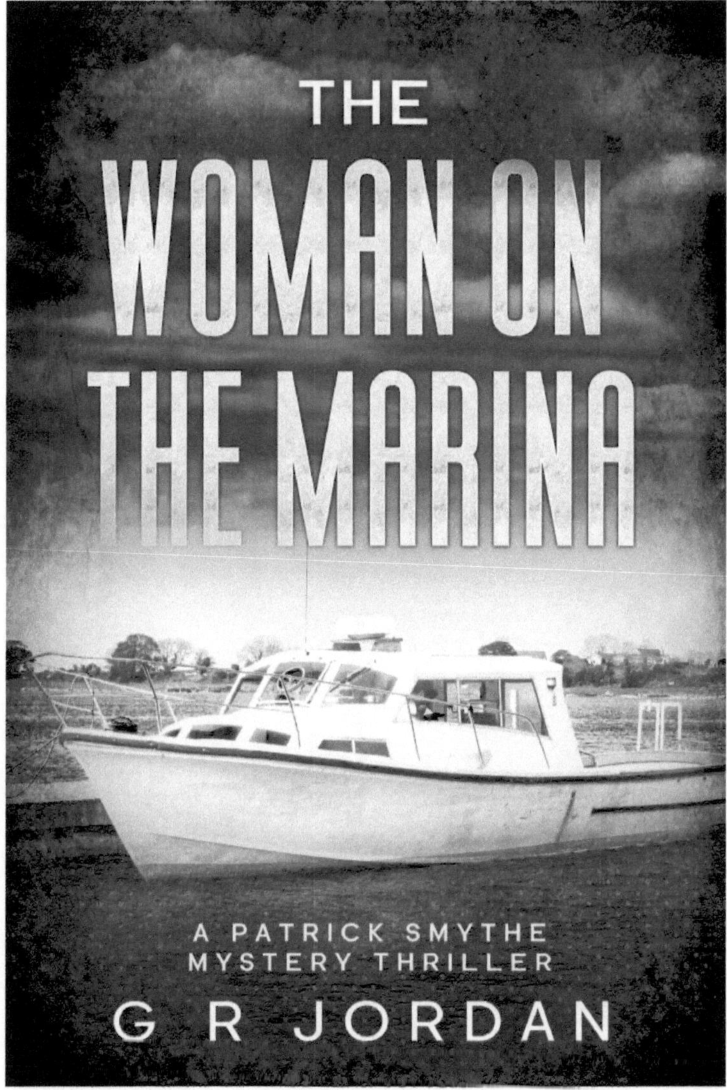

Patrick Smythe is a former Northern Irish policeman who after suffering an amputation after a bomb blast, takes to the sea between the west coast of Scotland and his homeland to ply his trade as a private investigator. Join Paddy as he tries to work to his own ethics while knowing how to bend the rules he once enforced. Working from his beloved motorboat 'Craigantlet', Paddy decides to rescue a drug mule in this short story from the pen of G R Jordan.

Join G R Jordan's monthly newsletter about forthcoming releases and special writings for his tribe of avid readers and then receive your free Patrick Smythe short story.

Go to https://bit.ly/PatrickSmythe for your Patrick Smythe journey to start!

About the Author

GR Jordan is a self-published author who finally decided at forty that in order to have an enjoyable lifestyle, his creative beast within would have to be unleashed. His books mirror that conflict in life where acts of decency contend with self-promotion, goodness stares in horror at evil, and kindness blindsides us when we at our worst. Corrupting our world with his parade of wondrous and horrific characters, he highlights everyday tensions with fresh eyes whilst taking his methodical, intelligent mainstays on a roller-coaster ride of dilemmas, all the while suffering the banter of their provocative sidekicks.

A graduate of Loughborough University where he masqueraded as a chemical engineer but ultimately played American football, Gary had worked at changing the shape of cereal flakes and pulled a pallet truck for a living. Watching vegetables freeze at -40'C was another career highlight and he was also one of the Scottish Highlands "blind" air traffic controllers.

These days he has graduated to answering a telephone to people in trouble before telephoning other people to sort it out.

Having flirted with most places in the UK, he is now based in the Isle of Lewis in Scotland where his free time is spent between raising a young family with his wife, writing, figuring out how to work a loom and caring for a small flock of chickens. Luckily, his writing is influenced by his varied work and life experience as the chickens have not been the poetical inspiration he had hoped for!

You can connect with me on:

🌐 https://grjordan.com

https://facebook.com/carpetlessleprechaun

Subscribe to my newsletter:

✉ https://bit.ly/PatrickSmythe

Also by G R Jordan

G R Jordan writes across multiple genres including crime, dark and action adventure fantasy, feel good fantasy, mystery thriller and horror fantasy. Below is a selection of his work. Whilst all books are available across online stores, signed copies are available at his personal shop.

Wild Swimming (Highlands & Islands Detective Book 40)
https://grjordan.com/product/wild-swimming
A remote sea cave reveals a grim discovery. A famous open-water swimmer's body stashed away. Can DCI Macleod stay afloat in an investigation where everyone seems to be in over their head?

When the body of a celebrated open-water swimmer is found in a secluded sea cave, DCI Macleod must navigate treacherous currents of rivalry, ambition, and fierce competition. As the investigation plunges into the dark depths of the victim's past, Macleod races against the tide to unmask a killer who moves like a shark in murky waters. Will he sink or swim in this case, where every competitor seems to have a motive and a watertight alibi?

In the world of open-water swimming, not everyone makes it back to shore!

Kirsten Stewart Thrillers
https://grjordan.com/product/a-shot-at-democracy
Join Kirsten Stewart on a shadowy ride through the underbelly of the Highlands of Scotland where among the beauty and splendour of the majestic landscape lies corruption and intrigue to match any city. From murders to extortion, missing children to criminals operating above the law, the Highland former detective must learn a tougher edge to her work as she puts her own life on the line to protect those who cannot defend themselves.

Having left her beloved murder investigation team far behind, Kirsten has to battle personal tragedy and loss while adapting to a whole new way of executing her duties where your mistakes are your own. As Kirsten comes to terms with working with the new team, she often operates as the groups solo field agent, placing herself in danger and trouble to rescue those caught on the dark side of life. With action packed scenes and tense scenarios of murder and greed, the Kirsten Stewart thrillers will have you turning page after page to see your favourite Scottish lass home!

There's life after Macleod, but a whole new world of death!

Jac's Revenge (A Jac Moonshine Thriller #1)

https://grjordan.com/product/jacs-revenge

An unexpected hit makes Debbie a widow. The attention of her man's killer spawns a brutal yet classy alter ego. But how far can you play the game before it takes over your life?

All her life, Debbie Parlor lived in her man's shadow, knowing his work was never truly honest. She turned her head from news stories and rumours. But when he was disposed of for his smile to placate a rival crime lord, Jac Moonshine was born. And when Debbie is paid compensation for her loss like her car was written off, Jac decides that enough is enough.

Get on board with this tongue-in-cheek revenge thriller that will make you question how far you would go to avenge a loved one, and how much you would enjoy it!

A Giant Killing (Siobhan Duffy Mysteries #1)

https://grjordan.com/product/a-giant-killing

A body lies on the Giant's boot. Discord, as the master of secrets has been found. Can former spy Siobhan Duffy find the killer before they execute her former colleagues?

When retired operative Siobhan Duffy sees the killing of her former master in the paper, her unease sends her down a path of discovery and fear. Aided by her young housekeeper and scruff of a gardener, Siobhan begins a quest to discover the reason for her spy boss' death and unravels a can of worms today's masters would rather keep closed. But in a world of secrets, the difference between revenge and simple, if brutal, housekeeping becomes the hardest truth to know.

The past is a child who never leaves home!

www.ingramcontent.com/pod-product-compliance
Lightning Source LLC
Chambersburg PA
CBHW051305210726
48287CB00002B/679